In Search of Herne the Hunter

By Eric L. Fitch

In Search of Herne the Hunter

©1994 Eric L. Fitch

ISBN 1 898307 23 7

ALL RIGHTS RESERVED

No part of this publication may be reproduced, stored in a retrieval system or transmitted in any form or by any means, electronic, mechanical, photocopying, scanning, recording or otherwise without the prior written permission of the author and the publisher.

Cover illustration by Sue Mason
Cover design by Daryth Bastin

Published by:

Capall Bann Publishing
Freshfields
Chieveley
Berks
RG16 8TF

Contents

Foreword	i
Chapter 1 .. .. .. The Legend	1
Chapter 2 .. .. .. The Thunder Tree	23
Chapter 3 .. .. .. Great Ragg'd Horns	41
Chapter 4 .. .. .. The Horned One	56
Chapter 5 .. .. .. The Devilish Chase	73
Chapter 6 .. .. .. The Mask of the Beast	92
Chapter 7 .. .. .. Death and Sacrifice	108
Chapter 8 .. .. .. A Fiendish Phantom	124
Chapter 9 .. .. .. The Web of Herne	137
Appendix A	145
Appendix B	149
Appendix C	153
Appendix D	155
Appendix E	157
List of Dates	159
Bibliography	162
Index	166

Acknowledgements

For help in the preparation of this book, I should like to thank Michael Bayley and Michael Shallis for their permission to relate their stories; T.M. for the illustrations of the Herne story; Eric Mottram for permission to reproduce his poem "Windsor Forest"; Rhiannon Ryall for permission to reproduce the Herne chant; Chesca Potter for her illustration "Herne the Hunter"; Michael Bayley again for permission to photograph his piece of Herne's Oak and for his illustration of the Mask of Herne; The Crown Estate Office for their assistance concerning Herne's Oak and Windsor Great Park; The British Museum; St. Albans Museum; Nationalmuseet, Denmark; Service Photographique de la Reunion des Musees Nationaux, France; Robert Hale Publishers; Fortean Picture Library; Windsor Public Library; and last, but not least, my wife Valerie for typing so many drafts.

Foreword

There cannot be many inhabitants of the Windsor area who are not familiar with their most famous ghost - Herne the Hunter - said to haunt Windsor Great Park wearing antlers upon his head and presaging national disaster. To local children he is their bogeyman used as a threat by parents to keep them in order. But to the wider public he is known from Shakespeare's reference to him in "The Merry Wives of Windsor" and from W. Harrison Ainsworth's novel "Windsor Castle".

The latter features Herne as a character, and during one scene he is described thus: "...... a weird figure, mounted on a steed as weirdlooking as itself, galloping through the trees with extraordinary swiftness. This ghostly rider wore the antlered helmet described by the Earl of Surrey, and seemed to be habited in a garb of deer skins. Before him flew a large owl, and a couple of great black dogs ran beside him." Herne also carried a hunting horn which, when he put it to his lips, issued forth bright blue flames and thick smoke, and he was sometimes accompanied by snakes and "a swarm of horribly grotesque, swart objects, looking like imps". A vivid picture indeed.

There may be a touch of romantic embellishment here, but Ainsworth's retelling is no doubt based on earlier tradition, the origins of which this book attempts to recover. In the process, the search explores the supernatural and the misty past as well as making some detours en route. By the end of the last chapter, however, I hope that some idea of the nature of Herne will have been conveyed and that you too will have become as captivated as I with the legend of Herne the Hunter.

Herne the Hunter by Chesca Potter

The Legend

> There is an old tale goes that Herne the Hunter,
> Sometime a keeper here in Windsor Forest,
> Doth all the winter-time, at still midnight,
> Walk round about an oak, with great ragg'd horns;
> And there he blasts the tree, and takes the cattle,
> And makes milch-kine yield blood, and shakes a chain
> In a most hideous and dreadful manner.
> You have heard of such a spirit, and well you know
> The superstitious idle-headed eld
> Receiv'd, and did deliver to our age,
> This tale of Herne the Hunter for a truth.

Thus did Mistress Page, in Act 4 Scene 4 of Shakespeare's "The Merry Wives of Windsor", describe Herne the Hunter. The play had its premiere in Windsor on 23rd April, 1597 and this is therefore the earliest recorded reference to Herne. It is also the most authentic we possess, despite its brevity, and all subsequent versions represent either romantic embellishments of Shakespeare, oral tradition handed down over generations or a combination of both.

Nevertheless, in order to get at the roots of Herne's story, as well as these sources I am going to base much of the discussion in this volume on W. Harrison Ainsworth's novel "Windsor Castle" of 1843. Although Ainsworth's telling of the tale is regarded largely as fiction, I believe that some of it must derive from local sources since it contains so many mythical themes which have much in common with other folk tales and pagan mythology. These themes, I believe, are so well interwoven into the legend that it is too much of a coincidence that they should all appear in one story. Whether Ainsworth was borrowing from local oral lore, or whether he penned the story himself using themes he knew through his studies is not known. But here, then, is a condensed rendition of Ainsworth's version.

Back in the reign of Richard II there was in Windsor Forest a young

The Legend

Herne plunged his knife into the hart's throat

The Legend

keeper by the name of Herne, who worked on the King's estate. Herne was so expert in woodcraft and hunting, that the King always chose him to join his party when he wished to hunt. On such occasions Herne would be accompanied by his two black hounds and, together, there was no-one who could better them. So much so, in fact, that Herne was envied by the other keepers who tried to think of ways to discredit him. Thus, one day the King was out hunting with his usual entourage when they came across a stag with a fine set of antlers. As they pursued it, the King and Herne broke away from the rest of the party and gradually gained upon the animal, which suddenly stopped, turned around and gored the King's horse, which immediately threw its rider. The King himself would have been gored too, however, had not Herne flung himself between the two to receive the blow instead. Although badly wounded, Herne managed to kill the beast by stabbing his knife into its throat.

As Herne lay dying, the King promised that, should he recover, he would be promoted to head keeper, but Herne replied that it was only a grave that he would need and fell unconscious. The King immediately summoned the rest of the hunting party, who gathered round the prostrate figure of Herne, and promised a large reward to any person who could bring him back to life, but the keepers, secretly pleased at Herne's fate, only suggested putting him out of his misery.

It was then that a stranger on a black horse appeared, who dismounted, approached the King and announced that he could cure Herne, since he was skilled in the practice of medicine. The King replied that he thought he was a poacher and one of the keepers claimed that he recognised him as such. However, the stranger said his name was Philip Urswick and that he lived on Bagshot Heath, where he had joined the chase that day. The keepers swore that they had not seen him join them, but the King interjected saying that he would reward him and give him a free pardon for whatever offences he may have committed, if he effected a cure for Herne.

Urswick agreed and to the keepers' surprise proceeded, with the aid of his hunting knife, to cut the antlers and skull from the stag and ordered

The Legend

My name is Philip Urswick

them to be tied onto Herne's head. He then ordered a stretcher to be made from branches and twigs and told the keepers to transport Herne to his hut. He added that Herne would revive under his care and be back for work in one month's time. Upon their arrival the keepers continued to speak against Herne and, on noticing this, Urswick asked them what they would reward him with if he aided them in their revenge. As they had nothing to give him, they agreed, on his suggestion, to carry out the first request he made of them. In return he promised that, although Herne would recover, he would lose all his woodcraft skills.

As Urswick foretold, Herne returned after one month and the King presented him with a purse of gold coins, a silver hunting horn and a gold chain. In addition he placed Herne in lodgings in the Castle itself. However Urswick's other prophecy also came true. Herne appeared to lose all his skills at hunting and other woodcraft pursuits and, to the delight of the other keepers, the King decided to dispense with his services. At this Herne rode off only to be seen later with the antlers upon his head, wielding a chain and acting in a crazed manner, and was last seen disappearing into the Home Park. Later that day he was found by a pedlar hanging from an oak tree, but when the pedlar had fetched the keepers from the Castle, the body had gone. And that night, Herne's Oak, as it came to be known, was blasted by lightning during a terrible thunderstorm.

The keepers continued their occupations but, whoever was head keeper, both he and his colleagues all seemed to fall under Herne's spell and they too could do nothing right. So, to avoid the King's displeasure, they decided to consult Urswick, who told them that the only way to remove the curse was to go to Herne's Oak. They arrived at midnight, whereupon the ghost of Herne appeared to them, complete with antlers, and ordered them to return the following night with horses and hounds as if to hunt, after which he vanished. As arranged, the keepers reassembled the next night, whereupon Herne reappeared and jumped upon his old horse and rode off into the forest, the keepers riding after him. After several miles they stopped and the figure of Urswick suddenly appeared before them. He welcomed Herne and then

The Legend

The bleeding skull was fastened upon the head of Herne

reminded the keepers that it was time for them to honour their promise. He commanded them to serve Herne and become his hunting party, to which they readily agreed and swore an oath to that effect.

That night and for many nights after, the strange troupe hunted, gradually depleting the deer herds and committing unspeakable outrages until the King himself came to hear of it. He ordered the keepers to come with him to Herne's Oak so that he could encounter Herne and speak with him himself. At midnight they arrived to see Herne mounted on his horse. The King spoke to him asking him why he haunted the Park as he did, to which Herne replied that it was for vengeance. He added that it was because of the other keepers that he was now in such an unfortunate state and he said that the only way he would stop haunting during the King's reign would be if the King hanged the keepers on the tree where be took his own life. At which Herne disappeared.

The next day the King did as he was bid and he was troubled no more whilst he reigned, although after his death Herne resumed his Wild Hunt which has been seen over the centuries right up until our own.

Thus spake Ainsworth in a version which I shall endeavour to show contains recognisable themes from our pagan past. But first there are variations to the story which must be told here not only to provide further interest but to examine the sort of variances which come about in folk tradition and to see if they have any bearing on getting to Herne's origins. The first variation is from the pen of Ainsworth again, where his novel describes Herne's story in a brief and quite different way, which could well reflect a local oral tradition. In this, Herne was said to be bewitched by a nun whom he carried off to a cave in the forest, but in a jealous rage he killed her and, full of remorse, he committed suicide. This story also took place in Richard II's reign, but other versions place the events surrounding the legend in the reign of other monarchs, as we shall see.

A simple variation records that Herne was wounded by a stag which he eventually managed to kill, whereupon he became mad, tied a set of

The Legend

A litter was formed with the branches of trees

antlers to his head and then hanged himself from the oak. Another omits the stag altogether and puts the suicide down to disgrace after committing some criminal deed. Others attribute this disgrace to hunting without permission, resulting in his betrayal to the King. After hanging himself his ghost, in the form of a stag, was said to haunt the oak, butt the trunk and tear at the roots whilst breathing fire and smoke. Two further stories place the events in the reign of Henry VIII. The first states that his suicide was due to his being suspected of witchcraft and that after his death his ghost was renowned for appearing to sentries at the Castle.

The second records that Herne hanged himself in despair after the king had defiled his daughter. This is the second version which features a sexual element, which we shall return to further on in our search. There is also a possible tradition that Henry V111 himself saw Herne. The 19c illustrator George Cruikshank once portrayed him appearing to the king, but whether Cruikshank knew of an authentic a tradition it is not possible to say. Yet another tale repeats the wounding of Herne by the stag and adds that he was driven mad with pain, whereupon he managed to kill the animal and, tearing off its antlers, he held them aloft and ran through Windsor Forest naked, before eventually hanging himself.

A different version again has Herne visit a wise woman in Eton after his goring, who advises him that if he wishes to be cured he must wear the antlers upon his head for one month. Elizabeth I's reign is the last backdrop and under her rule Herne is meant to have broken the strict forest laws, which usually resulted in torture or death. Rather than accept this, Herne hanged himself, after which he was said to appear beneath the oak along with a white stag.

So this sums up the evidence for the legend of Herne the Hunter and it can be seen that there are many variations on a central theme. That Shakespeare made use of oral tradition from the Windsor area seems certain, since many local names and places which are known to be relevant to Windsor have also been incorporated into the "The Merry Wives of Windsor". In addition, a pirate edition of the play, dating from 1602, includes another quote concerning Herne which is worth

The Legend

The king presented Herne with three gifts

The Legend

recording:

> Oft have you heard since Horne the hunter dyed,
> That women to affright their little children,
> Ses that he walkes in shape of a great stagge.

This would seem to be a record of an authentic tradition, the threatening of children with a local bogeyman being a universal practice. Shakespeare made much use of legends and folklore in his plays and thus the figure of the antlered Herne is not an unusual image to find. Indeed there is another reference to the wearing of antlers in "As You Like It". It is Act 4 Scene 2 and the following is sung by a character named Jacques:

> What shall he have that kill'd the deer?
> His leather skins and horns to wear.
> Then sing him home.
> Take thou no scorn to wear the horn,
> It was a crest ere thou wast born.
> Thy father's father wore it;
> And thy father bore it.
> The horn, the horn, the lusty horn,
> Is not a thing to laugh or scorn.

This verse celebrates the killing of a stag and as such is a celebration of victory. However, antlers were also used in folk custom as a symbol of adultery, the cuckolded husband being presented with a set when it was discovered that his wife had been unfaithful.

It is interesting to note the spelling of Herne - Horne - in the pirate version of the play. It may be a copying error, it could be that Horne was the original of Herne or it may be referring to an event recorded in a manuscript held in the British Museum. Dating from the time of Henry VIII, it tells of a Rycharde Horne, a yeoman, who was amongst a number of hunters who confessed to hunting illicitly in the royal forest. It has been put forward that this Horne was the origin of the Herne legend, and it may be that his story became confused in the popular

The Legend

Herne was found hanging from the branch of an oak tree

mind with Herne. Perhaps there is a grain of truth here and, if so, then it is similar to the case of Robin Hood, whose story contains much older elements which become attached to a later historical figure. Much could be said in a similar vein about King Arthur, whose legendary exploits owe a lot to Celtic myth.

Herne, Hearn or Hurne are not uncommon surnames and there is an example going back to 1279 where a Henry en le Hurne is recorded in the Berkshire hundred rolls. The name derives from a place-name, as discussed below, but Herne's name in the legend has been subject to different interpretations. An unlikely origin is the theory that Herne the Hunter was a drunkard, his name deriving from his drinking-horn, but the evidence for this is negligible.

As to the word "Herne" itself, we have seen that it may once have been spelt as "Horne", and perhaps it may be useful to examine some other names containing the core of "hern" or "horn". (For those unfamiliar with linguistics, it must be pointed out that the letters h and c are interchangeable between Indo-European languages, to which group most of the European languages belong.) To start with the pure form of Herne, we find this in place-names in both Kent and Hampshire, where the origin is the Saxon word "hyrne" meaning a corner or angle, whereas that in Bedfordshire derives from the Saxon "harum", dative plural of "haer" meaning a stone. A similar derivation is that of Cerne Abbas in Dorset which also means stone or rock, but in this instance derives from the Celtic "carn". It is appropriate here to note that Cerne Abbas also has its legendary figure, the huge chalk giant on the hillside above the village. However, it is "hyrne" which seems to be the most promising, the corner or angle normally referring to a bend in a river. It could well be connected with the Saxon word "horn", meaning a horn or horn-like hill as in Horne in Surrey, although Horne in Rutland derives from the Saxon "horna" meaning a corner or bend. This aspect of curvature in both derivations seems to be the key with the Herne of legend, as it is the curved nature of his horns or antlers which is of importance.

The Saxon "horn" is cognate with the Latin "cornu", which also means

The Legend

Herne appears to the king at the fated oak

horn. Nearly all European languages are connected and derive ultimately from one Indo-European language, thus it is possible to see similarities, despite phonetic changes (which can be identified), when comparing one language with another. Thus we come to one of the most important connections with Herne, in the form of the Celtic god Cernunnos. As can be immediately seen, it begins with the core "Cern" and the special relevance of this here is that Cernunnos was the horned god, often depicted with antlers (the horned god will be considered at length in chapter 4).

There is a possibility that the Cerne Abbas giant was once horned, thus linking him too with Cernunnos and providing an alternative origin for the village's name. That his club is in the shape of an oak leaf may well be significant, a topic which will be pursued further in the next chapter. It is of interest to note that the name of Cornwall in both its English version and its Cornish (Kernow) also contain this element which refers to the corner, curved shape or horn-like aspect of the principality itself. Thus here we see Horn - Herne - Cernunnos - Kernow - Cornu, all aspects of the one theme of the curved horn. It is therefore no surprise to find that a ghostly figure who wears a set of horns or antlers on his head is known by the name of Herne.

However, Andrew Collins widens the field and provides us with two further possible explanations for the origin of Herne's name. The first concerns place-names such as Herne Hill near Dulwich and Herongate in Essex; where the derivation is from the word "heron". Localities such as these were once the site of heronries and this may have a bearing on Windsor's Herne, as not far from his oak was once situated one of these breeding places known locally as the Heronry which was also near an area of woodland named Heron's Wood. Support for this hypothesis comes from an old dialect world "hern" or "herne" which means a heron and from the fact that a heronry was also sometimes referred to as a hernery. Thus it may be that Herne's Oak derived its name from the adjacent heronry, thereby passing it on to Herne himself.

According to Robert Graves the heron was a taboo bird in ancient times, along with the stork, cuckoo, lapwing and other species, which meant

The Legend

that, like the horse, it was a sacred animal not to be eaten or harmed in any way. Perhaps its veneration was partly due to its habit when collecting fish for its young to arrange its catch on the river bank in the shape of a wheel, tails touching. This has been explained as making it easy for the bird to pick up the fish and take them to its nest, but Graves, who once witnessed the phenomenon as a boy, viewed it differently. He saw the circular arrangement of fish as symbolising the sun and thence a king's life, an idea which dates back to ancient mythology. This, it will be recalled, is a central theme in the Herne legend, the king being saved from certain death by his brave forest keeper, and will be returned to in Chapter 7.

The heron's special reverence by early peoples seems to have endured the centuries, for Daniel Defoe recorded in his "Tour through the Island of Great Britain" of 1724 an old Sussex belief concerning the bird. It was thought that whenever the current Bishop of Chichester was about to die, a heron was seen to perch on the cathedral. And so we see that the heron has its place in British folklore and it may have been an element in the birth of the Herne legend.

Collins' second explanation takes us further afield to the Balkans, for it is in this region, especially around Thrace, that many monuments have been found which may have an indirect influence on the development of the Herne legend. Carved in stone, these monuments depict a figure of a horseman wearing a trailing cape and wielding a club or double-axe. Known as the Thracian rider, he is often found in Roman sanctuaries and is sometimes shown as part of a hunting scene, but what is most pertinent is the name often carved on the monuments - Heros or Heron. He was also a god of the dead, in which guise he was depicted on funerary monuments, and one of his legendary achievements was the conquering of a monster. His appearances on Egyptian monuments of the Roman period portray him offering a libation to a rampant snake.

And so the suggestion is that this Roman hunter god may well have been brought to our shores by the legionaries and his cult merged with that of Cernunnos. Indeed, it appears that the cavalry adopted him as their patron deity and altars to Heron have been discovered in western

Europe, although not in Britain, as far as I have been able to ascertain. The Romans brought various mystery cults with them to the British Isles, perhaps the most well known being those of Mithras and Isis. The former was well established here, with surviving temple remains in London and on Hadrian's Wall. Thus it is quite possible that the worship of Heron was also brought to Britain.

Whether this was indeed the case is difficult to confirm. Collins sees Heron as a hunt leader equating with Mars, who was also depicted on occasion as a rider with a club and sometimes bearing horns. This denotes the god of war as a fertility deity and one of his epithets - Rigonemetis, which means "of the sacred grove" - may indicate a role as Lord of the Forest and so a god of vegetation and woodlands. We shall examine this theme with reference to Herne later. As further evidence Collins cites various psychic communications which conjure the name of Heron in connection with discarnate woodland spirits and Heron place-names, but they do not add any real evidence for the presence of the Thracian rider in Britain.

Returning to Berkshire there are those who claim that Herne's name is uttered by the deer in the Park. At dusk and dawn their braying is heard by some to sound like voices calling "Herne, Herne". The stag, of course, plays an important part in the Herne legend and stag hunting was always a royal pastime. King James I, for instance, was especially fond of the chase and was well pleased on becoming king to find Windsor Great Park well stocked with deer. It is said that when a stag had been felled he quickly cut its throat and ripped open its belly, after which he would wallow in its blood which he would then commence to daub over his fellow hunters. A report from the Windsor Express of 9th November, 1838 gives a vivid description of a hunt when Queen Victoria's staghounds were led a merry chase by an old stag who apparently was so well known he had been named St. George. Deer have been a feature of Windsor Forest for centuries and there have always been deer in Windsor Great Park except for a period from 1951 to 1979. So important were deer to the area that there was once a chapel in the Park which was decorated with antlers.

The Legend

Windsor Forest used to be known as the Frith, meaning a deer park, and originally it had a circumference of 120 miles, although it was much reduced by the time of enclosure, 1813, when it then measured only 56 miles and it now contains some 7,000 acres. The early kings all enjoyed hunting and King Canute, perhaps, was the first to make laws concerning the regulation of hunts. Both Kings Edward and Harold had their deer-folds, which were enclosed areas of parkland, and the Norman monarchs were responsible for a law which decreed that only the king could own a forest, no doubt to control hunting which took place therein. It appears that during times of war, forests were cut down at an alarming rate, but there were some new plantations made. One of the earliest recorded was in Windsor Great Park in 1580, when some thirteen acres were sown with acorns and by 1625 the area had grown into a wood of tall young oaks. It had been necessary to fence the woodland off in the early stage, to prevent damage by cattle and deer.

By the Second World War, the deer in the Park numbered over one thousand, mainly red deer and a smaller number of fallow and, as their browsing could interfere with food production in the Park (needed for the war effort), it was decided that something had to be done. During 1940-41 seven hundred were culled and about three hundred were kept in an enclosed compound with a high fence, covering about 300 acres. After the war, King George VI decided that, as rationing was to continue for some time yet and the country needed all the food it could produce, the remaining deer had to go to free the land. So during 1950-51 they were transferred to Richmond Park, Badminton and Balmoral. Thus the Park remained without deer until they returned in February, 1979, a herd of red deer being reintroduced from Balmoral, and they now number some 500. They are again a common sight and even if you are unlucky enough not to see any whilst walking through the Park, you are certain to see the tracks they leave behind them.

The deer features to a large extent in British mythology, especially in the form of the White Hart or Hind, which was sacred to the Druids of Britain. Both Pwll, Lord of Dyfed and Sir Galahad of the Arthurian chronicles are said to have had encounters with white stags, whose appearances usually led mythical heroes into otherworldly realms. There is one amusing incident in Malory's Morte d'Arthur which is set in Windsor and involves Sir Lancelot, who often visited the town where Arthur sometimes held court. Whilst there he had got into the habit of resting by a well in the Great Park, where he would sometimes fall asleep, which he did on this occasion. However, it happened that a lady, accompanied by her retinue, was out hunting and had given chase to a hind. She let fly an arrow but it missed her quarry and ended up in Lancelot's buttock! The wound soon healed and it was not long before he was off to a tournament.

The stag was held to be a symbol of royal authority by the Saxons, which is exemplified by the bronze stag found to crown the standard from the royal ship-burial at Sutton Hoo in Suffolk. They also called their god Woden by the name of "stag" or "elk", but we shall be hearing more about him in later chapters. Of great significance, however, is the fact that Richard II himself - he of the Herne legend - adopted the White Hart as his personal emblem, perhaps giving rise to the many inn-signs up and down the country.

Mythologically, the White Hart symbolizes the goddess whose pursuit represents the luring of the horned god into her sacred grove. Moving on into Christian times, we encounter St. Eustace, a Roman general who was converted to Christianity after seeing a shining cross between the antlers of a stag he was hunting. He was later martyred for his faith. His feast day is 2nd. November, which is at the period of the Celtic festival of Samhain, when time is abolished and the barriers between living and the dead are broken down. We shall return to this theme later. An English saint, St. Tewdric, who led a hermit existence near Tintern, is said to have been borne upon a funeral bier pulled by two stags, as was Edward II. An Irish saint, St. Cainric, received assistance from a stag, which used to hold a book in its antlers whilst he read, and a stag led another Irish saint, St. Ciaran, to his future retreat upon an island in the middle of a lake.

A stag hunt forms the basis of a moral tale dating back to the reign of the Saxon king Edmund, who liked to stay at his royal residence at

The Legend

Cheddar in Somerset. At this time Dunstan held sway at the great abbey of Glastonbury, but the power and influence he wielded made the king's counsellors and nobles jealous and they succeeded in persuading their monarch to dismiss the unfortunate abbott.

Not long after this the king was leading a hunt through the Mendip forest and, in pursuit of a stag, the king broke away from the rest of the hunting party and his horse sped ahead in uncontrolled excitement. Edmund then saw the stag suddenly make a great leap and disappear over the cliffs of Cheddar Gorge. His horse, however, was in full gallop and could not be stopped and the king could see his death looming ahead. All of a sudden he recalled his treatment of Dunstan and he made a speedy oath to make amends if God would save him. And arriving at the cliff edge, Edmund's horse came to an abrupt halt, thus saving both their lives. Upon returning to his palace Edmund called for Dunstan and reinstated him to the Glastonbury abbacy. Thus we see stags weaving their way in and out of the legends and folk tales of the British Isles.

The stag and its associations with the royal chase at Windsor eventually led to its adoption as part of the emblem of Berkshire, along with the oak tree, and as described, both the stag and the oak play crucial roles in Herne's story. It therefore appears that they must have been of the utmost importance for many centuries in the Berkshire area. No doubt the oaks of Windsor Forest were familiar to and beloved by the inhabitants of the county, but there may be more to it than this. The oak, as we shall see in the next chapter, was a tree of special importance and in particular to the Druids, those priest figures of the iron-age Celts.

It may well be that Herne, or his ancestor Cernunnos, was worshipped in an oak grove in Celtic times and a possible derivation of the name Berkshire may add weight to this. The accepted origin is from the Celtic "barro" meaning a hilltop, but there is the possibility that it in fact derives from the Anglo-Saxon word "bearu" meaning a grove. Thus with the addition of the Anglo-Saxon for oak - "ac" - we end up with "bearu-ac-scire" or grove-oak-shire. Both the Celtic and Germanic peoples made use of sacred groves in their worship and it could well be that such a grove in Windsor Forest was held in high esteem and that this reverence continued into Christian times and persisted into the realm of folklore, together with folk memories of the horned god once worshipped there.

Herne is by no means the only example of such a folk-tale, as this one from Switzerland reveals. The story goes that a keeper once hanged himself from an oak tree in a forest near the town of Wildegg, and when his body was discovered by the local lord he instructed that the tree be cut down. However, upon receiving the axe blows, the tree began to ooze blood and so both the tree and the body were burnt. And ever since, the keeper's ghost has haunted the forest, being known as the Wild Huntsman of Wildegg, hunting with his spectral hounds. We are therefore seeing here themes which relate not only to Herne but to other traditions also, which will be explored as we proceed.

The scene has now been set for our quest for Herne the Hunter. As indicated in this introductory chapter, there are many aspects which are raised by the Shakespeare and Ainsworth writings, some of which have been touched upon already. However, it is pagan myth that this book is largely concerned with, and it will be necessary to enter into a web of interlinked ideas that make up the background upon which the Herne legend is based. I believe that the literary versions need to be taken seriously, even though there is a fair amount of romance in the case of Ainsworth. However, there is enough to suggest that the story does have a basis in mythology and folklore and my intention is to untangle the web and attempt to arrive at the origins of the legend. So it is time now to commence the search and to see where it leads us.

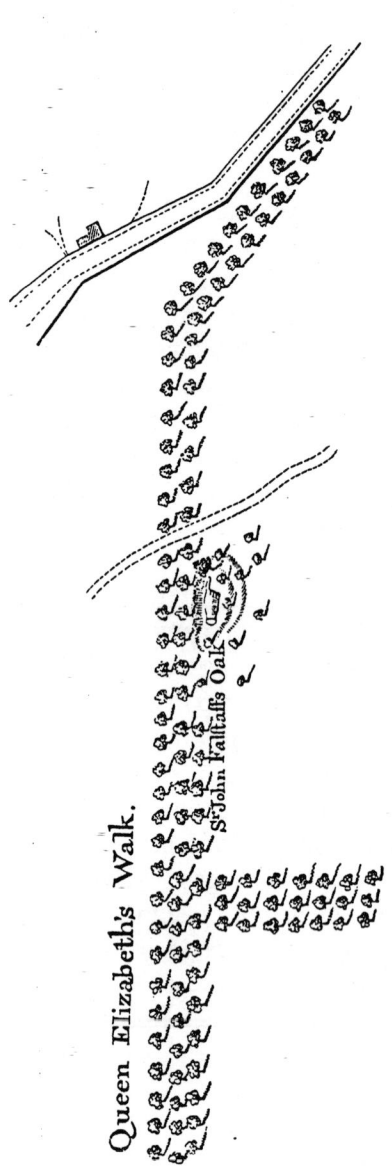

Part of a map of the Home Park in 1742, showing Sir John Falstaff's Oak

The Thunder Tree

Herne's Oak was cut down in the spring of 1796 at the unwitting order of George III who had commanded that all the trees be numbered that grew in the Little Park, now the private section of the Home Park. However his bailiff pointed out that some of the trees were in fact dead, which led to the King's order to have them felled. Unfortunately, Herne's Oak was amongst them and suffered the same fate. Upon discovering this terrible mistake, the King was apparently very sorry, for the ancient oak was highly regarded not only by himself but by the local townsfolk of Windsor. It had become a tourist attraction after the publication of "The Merry Wives of Windsor" and after Queen Elizabeth I had relaxed the laws relating to the royal parks. This enabled people to visit the Little Park more freely to view sites mentioned in Shakespeare's play. This freedom, however, was largely lost when James I ascended the throne and, wishing to hunt privately in the Great Park, had access to large areas forbidden. Nevertheless the local people regarded the Park as common land and no doubt many trespassers went unpunished.

The ancient oak itself was respected to such an extent that, after its felling, its "hard dark wood" was afterwards in much demand and was used for making items of furniture, tea caddies and other small articles, some of which have survived to this day. It was so sought after that the then president of the Royal Academy, Benjamin West, acquired a section of one of its knotty arms for himself. An ode to Herne's Oak was even composed (see Appendix A). There was also a local tradition that the spectral form of the tree was sometimes to be seen after its untimely demise, a ghostly tree haunting a fateful spot.

The search for the precise location of Herne's Oak has been outlined elsewhere (see Tighe & Davis, 1858) and a map of 1742 clearly marks the position of "Sir John Falstaff's Oak" adjacent to the edge of a pit. Interestingly this reference seems to indicate that the tree was known more for its appearance in Shakespeare's play than any tradition concerning Herne. No doubt the pit is that mentioned in the "Merry

*A piece of wood from the original Herne's Oak
(Courtesy of Michael Bayley)*

Wives of Windsor" where Nan Page and her "fairies" are "all couch'd in a pit hard by Herne's Oak". The pit no longer exists, as it was filled in sometime during the early 19c., but the site of the original tree now boasts a fine replacement, planted by Edward VII on January 29th, 1906, in memory of its venerable predecessor. Sketches made of the original tree show it to have been a pollard and these pictures, drawn in its final years, portrayed it in an advanced stage of decay and to be quite hollow. A report from a gentleman sometime after the felling of the tree stated that, when he was a singing boy at Windsor in 1786, he would often climb into the hollow of an old tree called Herne's Oak by his father, who was a native of nearby Datchet. Another local story claims that no grass would grow around the tree, a theme to be found attached to other strange localities such as Dragon's Hill near the Uffington White Horse. In 1783 the Oak produced its last acorns and in

1789 its last leaves. However, others were not of the opinion that this aged tree was Herne's Oak for, in 1838, another was cited as the real oak and upon being blown down in 1863, Queen Victoria had it replaced. This was removed when the real site was located in 1906 (see Appendix A).

This concern with a special oak tree is not unique and there are no end of other venerated oaks to be found throughout the length and breadth of the land. Indeed there was another in the Great Park itself called King's Oak, or the Conqueror's Oak, which was said to have been much admired by William the Conqueror. In fact its shell is still in existence and it has produced foliage every spring until recent times. Other examples include Major Oak in Sherwood Forest, where Robin Hood and his Merry Men used to meet; Augustine's Oak on the Isle of Thanet, where King Ethelbert received the missionary in 597; Turpin's Oak near Barnet, where the legendary highwayman hid in ambush; Reformation Oak in Norwich, where 20,000 men gathered in 1549 to repulse Royalist troops. The Carmarthen Oak was popularly associated with Merlin, giving rise to the couplet:

> When Merlin's Oak shall tumble down,
> Then shall fall Carmarthen town.

And more locally there is Druid's Oak in Burnham Beeches which, although probably over 500 years old, withstood the great storms of October, 1987 and January/February, 1990. Perhaps the most famous of all, though, is Charles' Oak in Boscobel Wood in Shropshire.

Tradition has it that it was in this tree that King Charles II hid in September, 1651 to avoid being captured by Cromwell, although the present tree was apparently grown from an acorn of the original, which had been chopped up by souvenir hunters. Upon the restoration of Charles II to the throne on May 29th, 1660, Oak Apple Day was inaugurated to celebrate the event, recalling to mind the help that the aforementioned tree gave to the king nine years earlier. This tradition involved adorning churches and houses with boughs of oak and the wearing of oak leaves, the custom in Berkshire involving wearing them in the buttonhole. However, it is probable that, like Guy Fawkes bonfires, the custom dates back into the distant past and is a continuation of pre-Christian rites. The oak flowers in May and it must be more than coincidence that this regenerative process took place around Oak-Apple Day. The oak was regarded as symbolic of summer in pagan times, no doubt due to its flowering at the height of the season and this special recognition continued into the Christian period. The Celts named one of their months after the tree. Duir (= oak) ran from 10th June to 7th July, in the middle of which came St. John's Day, June 24th, when the oakking was sacrificed (see Chapters 4 and 7). Thus, oak trees have been highly regarded for centuries in Britain and it is therefore appropriate to look at the background to the oak's prominence in the minds of men with a view to understanding why, perhaps, it was upon an oak that Herne hanged himself.

The most common native British oak is Quercus robur and is one of 300 types found in the temperate regions of the northern hemisphere. When the first settled communities in Britain emerged about six thousand years ago, much of the country was covered in thick oak forest. The tree was therefore very familiar to the neolithic farmers who cleared large areas of woodland by slashing and burning. However, the oak survived to become a special tree to our forbears and this is evidenced by the many placenames which incorporate the word "oak". Examples include Oake in Somerset, Oakhanger in Hampshire (oak slope), Okeford in Dorset (oak ford), Acklam in Yorkshire (oak wood) and Accrington in Lancashire (village where acorns grew).

Its wood is renowned for its strength, durability and elasticity and for these reasons was much used in British shipbuilding before the age of iron. It is said that, during the 18th. century, Admiral Vernon would traverse the countryside with his pockets loaded with acorns. He apparently planted them wherever he could so that there would always be a supply of oak wood with which to build more ships. In 1827 London Bridge was demolished to make way for a new one, and in the foundations were discovered some oak piles which were as sound as when they had been installed six or seven hundred years earlier.

The oak was venerated by virtually all ancient European peoples and was sacred to the various thundergods such as the Greek Zeus, Roman Jupiter, Celtic Taranis and the Germanic Thor. One of the most celebrated sanctuaries in the Greek world was that at Dodona in Epirus and there grew the oracular oak sacred to Zeus. It was here that the god's priestesses would listen to the rustling of the oak's leaves in order to hear the words of the oracle so that they could impart the answer to any question put to them. In keeping with its association with a thunder god, it was said that thunderstorms would rage at Dodona more frequently than anywhere else in Europe. The sight of a great oak struck by lightning is quite striking and it is therefore quite understandable that the ancients saw the oak as a channel whereby the thunder god would communicate to humankind.

The Old Testament confirms the pagan Gentiles' reverence of the oak, as this passage from Ezekiel (6.13) bears out:

"Then shall ye know that I am the Lord, when their slain men shall be among their idols round about their altars, upon every high hill, in all the tops of the mountains, and under every green tree, and under every thick oak, the place where they did offer sweet savour to all their idols."

Thus it is apparent that human sacrifice took place in sacred groves in the name of Baal.

The Germanic tribes were renowned for their holy groves and Tacitus, the Roman writer, refers to them in his "Germania". In the eighth century a tree known as Jupiter's Oak was cut down in religious zeal by a Christian missionary, St. Boniface, at Geismar in Germany, but paganism continued long after. The old German laws exacted a terrible punishment for those who committed the crime of peeling the bark of a tree. The offender's punishment was to have his navel cut out and nailed to the damaged part of the tree, after which he was made to walk round and round the tree until his intestines had wrapped themselves around the trunk. Thus living tissue replaced the wound the perpetrator had inflicted, a life for a life. The Prussians remained unconverted for many years after the rest of Germany and 16c. writers make reference to sacrifices they made in their sacred groves. Vestiges of such practices may also have lingered late in Britain for in 1538 a priest accompanied by an oaken idol were both burned at the stake at Smithfield.

This reverence has continued right up until the 20th. century. Even Nazi Germany recognised its importance for, at the 1936 Berlin Olympics, Adolf Hitler presented each competitor with an oak sapling. It was hoped that when each tree was planted it would remind the people of whence it had come.

The Greeks and Romans saw the acorn as the glans penis and thus regarded the oak as a fertility symbol. Reinforcing this was the respect shown to mistletoe growing on oak trees, the juice of which was regarded as seminal fluid and the Roman author Pliny recommended that women who wished to conceive should carry a sprig of mistletoe around on their person. The use of mistletoe at our Christmas celebrations no doubt reflects this ancient veneration, but its pagan and sexual overtones never allowed it to be accepted within the Church's festivities as were the holly and the ivy. Of course the idea of the Druid, which comes from the Celtic derwydd meaning "oakseer", dressed in white robes cutting the mistletoe from an oak with a golden sickle and catching it in a white cloak is well known. The village of Whiteleaved Oak by the Malvern Hills is thought by some to have been the site of such a sacred tree used long ago by the Druids. In fact mistletoe is rarely found growing on oak trees and it is probably this rare coupling of the plant which grows midway between heaven and earth with the thunder god's tree which made it so special.

In pre-Christian times couples were sometimes married beneath Marriage Oaks and remnants of this persisted into the Christian period when newlyweds would dance around such an oak and cut a cross in its bark. A notable example of the association of the oak and the Faith is to be seen at the Chapel Oak in Allanville, Normandy. Here grows a huge tree which contains within its hollow trunk an altar dedicated to the Virgin Mary, and it is still used on occasion for celebrating Mass.

The oak was also used for medicinal purposes and the Romans

dedicated it to Asculapius, the Greek Asclepius, the god of healing. When the sick were carried to his temple, attendants would walk before them bearing oak branches. In folk medicine various remedies were used which utilised different parts of the oak. Its bark was used in decoction for washing lacerations and the vapour emitted from an infusion of the bark apparently cured haemorrhoids. Red oak bark was included in a concoction which effected a cure for dysentry and bark boiled in skimmed milk provided a remedy for diarrhoea. Oak buds could be used both internally and externally for helping fevers, inflammation and effusions and grated acorns were also efficacious in curing various ailments.

Long life is indicated by dreaming of an oak tree and the oak is traditionally associated with hospitality. It also stood as a symbol of renewal, which has led various people to use its energies therapeutically. Bismark used to stand for half an hour leaning against an oak when feeling low and the North American Indians apparently renewed their energies in a similar manner. Psychics or sensitive people have even been known to hear an oak "singing". It is therefore a tree of much importance in the field of medicine and perhaps Urswick used oak in the curing of Herne and perhaps the foresters used oak branches when preparing his stretcher. The special nature of the oak may also explain why it is host to more kinds of animals and plants than any other species of British tree.

It was believed that when an oak was felled it groaned or shrieked and that to cut one down was considered sinful and very unlucky, but to keep its branches or acorns in a house protected it from being struck by lightning. However, oak wood became even more powerful if the tree it had come from had itself been struck, and to stand under an oak gave one protection not only from being struck by lighting but also from the power of witches. Oak was used for fuel at the Celtic fire festivals of Lughnasad (August 1st.), Samhain (November 1st.), Imbolc (February 1st.) and the most important, Beltane (May 1st.). The latter was held in honour of the solar god Bel or Belenos, whose name means "brightly shining" and the oak was sacred to him, being the midsummer tree, flowering at the sun's peak of intensity. The god was also associated with the fertility of cattle and there may well be a connection here with Herne in that Shakespeare tells us that he "takes the cattle and makes milchkine yield blood". The web of interconnectedness in folklore and mythology may be telling us that these themes of oak/horned god/fertility/cattle are originally parts of an early myth, and we shall see more of these links as our quest progresses.

Moving further back in time to the bronze age, we find another example of the veneration of the oak in the form of a burial from Gristhorpe in Yorkshire. Beneath a large burial mound was discovered in 1834 a large skeleton which had been placed in an oak coffin, hewn out of the trunk and split in two to form a base and a top. Above the coffin a quantity of oak branches had been placed together loosely. Here again we see the significance of the oak, this time dating from about three thousand years ago, and it was probably its strength and generative association which were in mind when the burial was made. Perhaps it was hoped that the man's soul would live on with the aid of the magical oak. It is probable that this rite continues a tradition which reaches back into the preceding neolithic period and we are therefore talking about a period of several thousand years in which the oak has been of prime importance.

The oak is not the only tree to have been held sacred, of course, and the worship of trees was general throughout Europe in early times. This could be expected considering that vast areas of the continent were covered with forests before deforestation began during the neolithic age. Trees were considered by ancient peoples to have souls just as humans, animals and other plants, and their cutting down had to be done with regard to their feelings. Initially they were thought to have been animated by a spirit which dwelt within them just as it did within humankind, but later it was thought that a supernatural entity made the

---

Footnote:- The Anglo-Saxon god Woden was equivalent to the Norse god Odin. Although the myths relating to the god are known mainly from those relating to Odin, I shall use the name Woden in all instances in this book for convenience.

The Thunder Tree

tree its abode, which eventually led to the idea of a god dwelling amongst the branches. An example illustrating this concerns the missionary Jerome of Prague who went amongst the pagan Lithuanians in order to bring them to the Faith, which included the felling of their sacred groves. However, a deputation of women appealed to their prince to stop him, claiming that he was desecrating the house of Perkunas, their god of thunder and lightning, responsible for bringing both sunshine and rain. The oak was especially sacred to Perkuna, one of whose duties was to pursue demons and he would disguise himself as a hunter to hound the Devil. It appears that as late as the 14c. the Lithuanians still consulted oak trees in their capacity as oracles.

Maypoles also originate in the pagan past and were originally actual trees felled in a woodland, brought to the village and around which the May ceremonies took place. Later, however, this gave rise to permanent maypoles being erected, a few of which survive to this day. Traditionally at May time came the figure of Jack in the Green or the Green Man. This figure clad in greenery upon a basketwork frame appeared at the May revels and represented the regenerative nature of spring.

Trees feature in much world mythology, perhaps none more so than the Norse Yggdrasil, the World Ash. This tree acted as a pivot upon which the heavens revolved and gnawing its roots was the Cosmic Serpent, perched at its top was the World Eagle and browsing amongst its branches was the stag Eikthyrni. It was the tree upon which the god Woden (see footnote) hanged himself which, as we shall see later, is a key myth in connection with Herne and his origins. Yggdrasil stood at the centre of the world and its branches reached out over heaven and earth. Of its three roots one passed into the realm of Woden's descendants, the Aesir, the second led to the land of the frost giants and the third into the land of the dead, thus acting as a link between these realms, humankind and the gods. The idea of the tree at the centre of the world was taken over by the Cross, but guardian trees, which stood adjacent to houses and temples, lingered on well into Christian times. Indeed, the Old Manor House at Knaresborough is built around such a tree, and it has been suggested that it was a tree which lay at the centre

The Thunder Tree

Herne's Oak by Samuel Ireland, 1790

of Stonehenge.

The image of the tree is a significant feature of shamanism. The word shaman translates as "one who knows" and refers to an individual who was responsible for the welfare of a tribe in that he would be healer, poet, prophet and guardian of his tribe's myths. During the shaman's ecstatic trances he ritually ascended a pole which acted as a substitute for the World Tree and which enabled him to gain access to the Otherworld. It was then that he was able to contact the spirit world and receive messages so that he could return with them for the benefit of the tribe.

In the nomadic tribes of northern Asia it is the belief that the heavens are held together by the "pillar of the world", often symbolized by a

Herne's Oak by Paul Sandby, c1785

stake being driven into the ground in the centre of the village. The sky is also regarded as a circular tent which needs support and the pillar which provides this support is also seen as a means whereby a shaman is able to ascend to the heavens. It is for this reason that when a shamanistic rite takes place a pole is erected in the middle of the tent with its top sticking out of the roof. This idea is connected with the desire to construct religious buildings such as towers or ziggurats which were seen to be the centre of the world and to reach to the sky above. Related to of this is the Tree of Life which grew in the middle of the Garden of Eden.

The concept of the World Tree or Tree of Life was widespread and from very early on it was linked with the death of a saviour, normally a god who then achieved immortality. This was specially so in Palestine, where the worship of sacred trees and pillars was common before the arrival of the Israelites, such trees being of religious importance to the Canaanite goddess Astarte. Although the Israelites later denounced such practices, the idea of the Tree of Life was by no means forgotten and in later Christian times its symbolism was taken over by the Cross upon which Christ was crucified. The Tree of Life is a key factor in Hebrew Cabalistic tradition and illustrates the underlying unity within the universe. It acts as a model connecting the universe with God and humankind, and the Tree's branches spread throughout creation reconciling the individual leaves and branches, which represent universal phenomena, with the unified overness of the whole.

Thus we can see that trees have enjoyed an intimate relationship with humankind over the centuries, so much so that they have become symbolic of regeneration, life, the universe and everything. The oak in particular has played a special role, especially in European mythology, and it is not insignificant that Herne hanged himself on such a tree. The links between Herne, his antlers and prehistoric religion will become apparent in later chapters and the oak will be seen to slot into the jigsaw that makes up Herne's story.

It can be pointed out here, though, that there is a connection with trees and antlers in that branches were often seen to assume the shape of antlers. Indeed, old trees used to be known as stagheaded, for the upper branches without leaves stood out in outline against the lower foliated ones, which gave the appearance of a stag's horns. No doubt Herne's Oak was in this state in its later years.

Continuing this theme of trees and antlers, there is a curious tale from the Lake District which combines the two major elements of the Herne legend - antlers and the oak tree. The story goes that in 1333 the King was out hunting one day at Whinfell, Westmorland, when his hound Hercules took after a stag and chased it to Redkirks in Scotland and back. On their return, however, the stag had to leap over a fence but died after it had done so. Hercules shared the same fate after he attempted, but failed, to clear the fence. Nearby stood an oak tree and, to commemorate the event, the stag's antlers were nailed upon it, whereupon it was known thence as the Hartshorn Tree. As with

Herne's Oak pieces from the tree seem to have been prized, as Lord Hothfield is reported as having such a piece on his writing table at Appleby Castle in 1922. Such is the magic of the oak.

The story of the spectral Herne's Oak appearing after its demise is an interesting example of the manifestation of a tree spirit. That trees contained spirits was believed by most ancient peoples, perhaps the most well known being the Dryads from Greek mythology, who were oak nymphs. There is a modern belief in some circles that all living organisms possess a "spirit" of sorts that can exist independently after that organism has died, giving rise to certain forms of ghost story. Trees are considered to be no exception and a tale told to me recently, and one I have no reason to disbelieve, illustrates the phenomenon well. A young lady took up residence in a new house and one night in bed

The Long Walk Windsor

The Thunder Tree

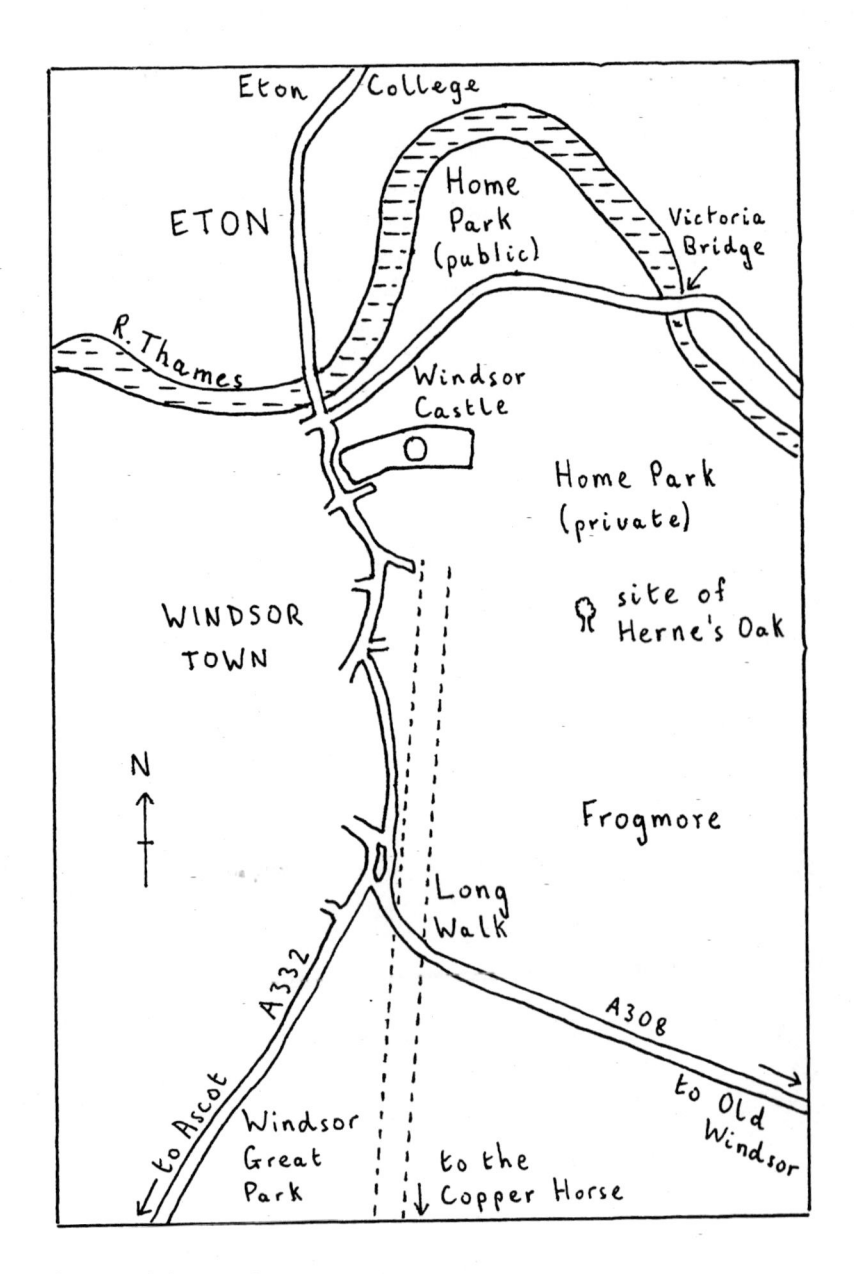

A map of the Windsor area, showing the position of Herne's Oak

woke up to see what she described as a figure dressed in a green suit standing near the foot of her bed, holding a staff and staring at the wall. Too terrified to speak and the door being on the other side of the figure she just stayed put until she fell asleep. This continued for some nights until she at last mentioned the occurrence to someone who suggested an answer. When she drew a picture of the figure to the acquaintance, he could see it took the form of what can only be described as a "Christmas tree man", in that the green suit appeared as the foliage of a fir tree. He immediately recognised it as a tree spirit and told her that if she consulted local records, she would probably find that a fir tree stood on the site where her house now stands. She researched the house's history and, of course, found this to be the case. Such ghostly phenomena seem only to be seen by those with psychic sensibilities, but perhaps this gift was once more common amongst the population. The ghostly form of Herne's Oak may well have appeared to many, before fading with time.

Which brings us to the siting of Herne's Oak in relation to the landscape around it. In ancient times, and up until modern days in the far east, the position of buildings and sacred sites was of crucial importance. The Chinese science of geomancy, or fengshui, provides us with some idea of this notion, which aimed at harmonising man with his environment. The earth and nature were considered as a living, breathing being, to which it was essential to be attuned if life were to be lived harmoniously and happily. Geomancers would be consulted whenever a building was to be erected in order that its positioning and orientation did not conflict with the underlying earth currents or dragon paths, as they were known in China, since they were supposed to be the flight paths of dragons on route between nests. There are still remnants of these ideas elsewhere in the world. In North American Indian culture they become creation paths, frequented by the primeval serpent, the ancestral guardian of all life forms. In Ireland they are fairy paths, said to be processional routes which ran along ancient tracks, where they were still visible at all. Tradition had it that on the day of a procession, a house which stood on such a path should have its front and back doors left open so as not to obstruct the fairies. We have seen that fairies were associated with Herne's Oak and the idea of the connection between oaks and fairies is remembered in an old couplet which states:

> Fairy folk
> live in old oaks.

Allied to these supernatural paths are what were known as hostpaths in Anglo-Saxon times. Often considered devilish, they were a memory of the routes taken by invading armies and which were remembered due to the rape and pillage which took place as the troops passed through. There were a fair number in Berkshire itself and some followed the course of Roman roads. The section of the Silchester-London road near Crowthorne is still known today as the Devil's Highway. The Wild Hunt (see chapter 5) is often associated with the path of an old Roman road and this may be the source of the straight lines recorded as being the route taken by the Hunt. The Devil's Highway is still traceable today as it passes just south of Virginia Water into the outskirts of Windsor Great Park and thus into Herne country.

These dragon, host and fairy paths have much in common with the idea of leys, those invisible but, to some, clearly marked lines which are said to crisscross the countryside. Although a controversial topic in archaeological circles, leys have been investigated by enthusiasts since their existence was suggested by Alfred Watkins in his book "The Old Straight Track", published in 1921. What interests us here is the fact that the site of the original Herne's Oak lies on such a ley. These lines are apparently indicated by sites such as burial mounds, standing stones, earthworks, churches and some leyhunters and dowsers are convinced that subtle energies are associated with the lines.

The ideas put forward for their existence have come a long way from Watkins' theory that they were merely tracks and recent research has connected them not only with supernatural occurrences such as ghosts but also with sightings of U.F.O.'s. In Germany, Geisterwegen or "ghost roads" are recorded, paths which are dead straight and which start or finish at a burial ground. Next door in Holland there are doodwegen or "death roads" which also terminate at cemeteries, along which corpses were transported. These types of pathway are now being linked to ideas of spirit paths, which were associated with various types of discarnate spirit, and the whole topic of leys is now under revision.

However the author Geoffrey Ashe, himself steeped in the legends of Britain, says "While alignments exist, and a few may be deliberate, the ley theory as a whole is a modern myth". On the other hand, geomancer Paul Devereux, perhaps the world's authority on leys, has championed their cause for many years and he now sees them as combinations of shamanistic spirit paths, some prehistoric alignments and many chance alignments. But the debate about their existence and their nature will continue for some time to come.

There are thought to be two leys running southwards from Windsor Castle. The first runs thus: the Round Tower - Albury Common (earthwork) - Chobham church - Losely House - Farncombe church - Hydon's Ball - Chiddingfold (Roman building). The second runs south east from the Round Tower - Great Fosters - St. Ann's Hill (earthwork) - Ockham Common (burial mound) - Westcott church - Rusper church. It is this second ley which is of interest to us since the site of Herne's Oak lies upon its line. This may well be of great significance, especially considering the fact that supernatural occurrences like ghostly manifestations are coming to be found more and more along leys. As described earlier, the Wild Hunt is sometimes said to follow a straight line, and perhaps this has contributed to the idea of leys as paths half-forgotten but remembered in folklore. Even more significant is the site of the Fairy Dell, mentioned in Shakespeare's "Merry Wives of Windsor" as being adjacent to Herne's Oak for, as we have seen, fairies were often associated with such ancient, mysterious trackways. Thus we have here a conglomeration of phenomena a ley, a venerated oak, a spectral figure and a fairy dell, which all add up to the area being very special, a place which has probably been sacred from early times.

This survey of the oak and its reverence reveals that it is likely that it is no mere coincidence that it was an oak upon which Herne hanged himself. That the oak was a sacred tree to the Celts, who also worshipped the horned god (see chapter 4), has been shown and it is

The Thunder Tree

apparent that it was also revered in prehistoric times before the Celts. Its association with the generative mistletoe and also lightning brings it into close contact with the gods and the mythology which surrounds figures such as Woden and world trees like Yggdrasil. Thus Herne's Oak and its relationships described in this chapter give us a first clue in joining up the jigsaw puzzle which makes the story of Herne the Hunter.

Great Ragg'd Horns

Thus did Shakespeare describe Herne's headgear, but what was the significance of the antlers? The horns of bulls have been revered in many cultures, such as Minoan Crete, and were symbolic of their owner's strength and power. The Cretans saw the bull as a symbol of masculine fertility and believed that the horns contained his vitality, probably due to their rapid growth. Their rites involved offering a bull's head complete with horns to the sky god. Horns were also associated with the moon, due to their similarity with the lunar crescent, and thus became linked to goddess worship. Antlers, however, were a special case due to their yearly renewal and idiosyncratic shape. To help understand the full significance of animals such as deer to early man and the special regard he had for their antlers, it will be necessary to delve into the realms of prehistoric archaeology and folk customs.

We begin with an ancient burial dating back to the dawn of modern humanity. In a cave called Jebel Qafzeh near Nazareth in Israel excavations have revealed fossil human remains of individuals who are anatomically the same as ourselves but who died about 100,000 years ago. Most remarkable was the skeleton of a boy aged about 12 or 13 who had been buried clutching a set of fallow deer antlers. Such a find seems to indicate a deliberate interment involving a belief in an afterlife of some sort, the antlers no doubt symbolising rebirth and new life. It is one of the earliest examples we have of ritual behaviour and it is highly appropriate to this study that antlers were used in religious practices at such an early date.

Moving forward to palaeolithic Europe during the last ice age, we visit the wonderful pictures painted inside the caves of Lascaux in France and Altimira in Spain. It is apparent from such cave paintings that the red deer was a major food source for these people as there are many depictions of this species amongst all the other animals which appear on the walls. Some picture them being hunted with bows and arrows, whilst others show them running or even swimming. Reindeer were also of prime importance and there are indications that there may have

Great Ragg'd Horns

Star Carr antler frontlet (British Museum)

been domesticated herds, which would have provided an abundant food supply. Thus from the earliest times European man has been in contact with antlered beasts and, as nothing went to waste in those far-off days, antlers were soon discovered to be of use both practically and ornamentally.

However, there are some worked antlers discovered in caves which have proved more mysterious and these are "wands" made of reindeer or stag antlers. They are T shaped and at the intersection are either one or two holes. The earliest date from the Aurignacian period (about 40,000 B.C.), but when the Magdalenian (15,000 - 10,000 B.C.) is reached they become ornate with engravings which can be quite intricate. Various suggestions have been put forward as to their use, such as tent pegs, arrowheads, ritual drumsticks, brooches and harnesses, but none of these is certain. Perhaps they had some religious purpose and were a symbol of power or status attached to some rite which we can now only guess at. Also found are cylindrical or, more often, semi-cylindrical "batons" with ornamental engravings carved upon them in the form of loops, circles and spirals, all of which were used in the later neolithic and bronze ages and may well represent the sun, moon and cycle of life. That they were carved on the regenerative antler probably suggests recognition of their special quality.

The earliest antlers found in Britain to have been fashioned by man are particularly relevant to the legend of Herne the Hunter. About 10,000 years ago in the mesolithic era, or middle stone age, a small band of hunter-gatherers settled one winter at Star Carr in the Vale of Pickering, Yorkshire. Here they set up a lakeside camp on a muddy slope where they constructed a platform of branches and brushwood which was used as a landing stage for their canoes. No doubt it also supported dwellings of some sort, perhaps made of reeds or animal skins. The attraction of the site was the potentional for fishing and for hunting other animals and birds which frequented the shore.

The importance of hunting to this community was apparent from the animal remains excavated from the site, the bones of many species

Great Ragg'd Horns

Reconstruction of antler head-dress from Star Carr (British Museum)

being present including deer (most numerous), aurochs, wolves, wild boars, foxes and beavers and also birds such as ducks, cranes and storks. The remains of elk, roe deer and red deer were prominent, the latter especially so with 102 antlers surviving, of which 83 had been cut to produce splinters used to make barbed points for spears or harpoons.

However, the relevance of Star Carr to this study is the survival of 21 stag skulls with parts of the antlers still attached. None was still intact and many of the antlers' beams had been broken off near the stump, nevertheless there were enough good examples to show that here was a unique collection. They had all been worked in such a way as to make them lighter. Much of the beam had been cut away and what was left had been hollowed out. The inside of the cranium had also been gouged to make the skull thinner and there was obviously an intention to remove as much of the weighty bone as possible. But what made these stag frontlets so intriguing were the two perforated holes made in each of the temples, which could only have been used for one purpose - to pass thongs through to enable them to be tied somewhere, presumably to someone's head.

So here we can envisage antlered figures looking out at us from the distant past, primeval forerunners of Herne himself. But as to the reason for donning these headdresses, there are two schools of thought. One is merely practical and suggests that the antlers were worn whilst hunting deer, perhaps being used as decoys. The Maidu Indians of California used antlers in this fashion, dressing themselves in deer skins, painting their chests white and tying a set of antlers onto their head. Attired thus they would approach the deer herds whilst rattling sticks together in imitation of the clashing of stags' antlers at mating time. A similar instance is that of the Inuit, or Eskimos, when hunting caribou. Here a hunter carries a pair of antlers above his head and imitates the mating grunts of the animal, which attracts the bulls. Thus there is a possibility that this may have been the purpose of the Star Carr antlers. However, the finding of so many together in one deposit hints at other uses.

The second view is of a ritual function for the headdresses, the suggestion being that they were worn, perhaps along with deerskins, during dances which were aimed at ensuring the abundance of the deer herds and/or the fertility of nature in general. Alternatively they may have been used in sympathetic magic to ensure good luck in hunting. The Taos Indians of the Rio Grande performed a winter hunting dance dressed in deer skins and with antlers on their heads. They would dance around the snow-covered, sacred Rocky Mountain, which they regarded as their Animal Mother, and the dance represented the hunted animals and their Mistress. The Yacqi deer dancers from Arizona and Mexico still portray a realistic mime of hunting and killing, adorned with a stag's skull and antlers upon their heads. It seems highly likely that the mesolithic dwellers at Star Carr would have had magical beliefs and it is not difficult to envisage them taking part in some form of ritual ceremony. Unfortunately, corroborative evidence in the form of other ritual deposits is sadly lacking, as mesolithic finds are few and far between.

Returning to the Continent, an excavation at Stellmoor in Germany produced a most interesting discovery. It appears that at the beginning of the mesolithic period about 10,000 years ago, a group of reindeer hunters camped at the edge of a lake, much in the same manner as their contemporaries at Star Carr. Although no stag frontlets were discovered here, what was unearthed was of special importance. Close to the shore a pinewood pole nearly seven feet long was found which was pointed at one end and blunt at the other, upon which was mounted a reindeer skull complete with antlers. Nearby were twelve more skulls with antlers, no doubt previous occupants of the end of the pole, and it appears that this ritual pole was stuck in the ground at the water's edge with the antlers on display. But what purpose did this prehistoric totem pole serve? We find the answer with the accompanying deposits discovered nearby.

Twelve whole reindeer had been submerged in the lake, all weighed down by having large stones placed in their abdomens. In addition the skulls of thirty others were found in association with large stones, signifying further ritual deposits. They seem to belong to young does, some possibly pregnant, which were offered to the lake deities.

Perhaps we can envisage a shaman slitting open the abdominal cavity with his flint knife, placing the stone within and then sewing it up again with sinew. Then amongst ceremonies which must remain a mystery to us, the animal is deposited in the lake. The development of the antlers tell us that this occurred around May/June and perhaps these people inaugurated the commencement of the season's hunting with the sacrifice of their first fruits. The fact that the victims were all female may have indicated hunting magic to ensure the plentiful supply of reindeer or, alternatively, the watery grave may signify some special significance for water, which has always been associated with fertility. But perhaps their god was thought to reside underground and the ritual deposit represented an attempt to make the offerings reach the deity. Whatever the precise reason, there is no doubt as to the preoccupation with deer and their antlers, a phenomenon which did not stop with these mesolithic hunters.

Moving onwards to the neolithic age, red deer antlers were used as picks and are common finds from sites such as the great circle-henge of Avebury and Grimes Graves flint mines. But these artefacts are not always the result of mere chance deposits thrown away after use. At the west end of what is known as the Lesser Cursus (an avenue of earthen banks and ditches) situated near to Stonehenge, several antlers were discovered. However, this was no random deposit, for each antler had been purposely buried in the ditch at regular intervals before the ditch was backfilled. Cursuses, some of which stretch miles across the countryside, are enigmatic features and all that can be said of them is that they appear to be of a ritual nature. They are often aligned to, or contain within their structure, long barrows and therefore a religious function seems to be their purpose. But there is still the question as to why antlers were placed at such sites and why they became such symbolic and magical objects.

The answer to this question lies in the growing and shedding of antlers and their rapid growth, increasing in size each year, must have been a source of wonder for ancient man. In Britain the indigenous species are the red deer and roe deer. The latter's antlers are small compared with the red deer's, whose antlers can grow up to twelve points, when

Great Ragg'd Horns

the animal is known as a royal stag. (Male deer alone bear antlers, except in the case of reindeer and caribou).

Antlers grow out of bony projections on the skull called pedicles. During the first year of growth they appear as points and, when they are shed, they become covered with skin which is richly supplied with blood vessels. It is from these that the antlers develop and the skin, which is covered with short hair, grows to cover the antlers completely until they are fully formed. Their purpose is for fighting in the rutting season, just before which the stags join the hind herds to engage in the annual battles.

This rapid yearly growth coupled with the use of the antlers during the mating season must have led to their veneration as sexual and fertility symbols from early times and the reason why they are found in ancient burials. At Chaldon Herring in Dorset an excavated barrow revealed a deeply cut grave containing the skeletons of two adults who had been buried either crouched or in a sitting position with antlers resting on their shoulders. Another similarly positioned skeleton, also with antlers was found in an adjoining barrow. A burial at Amesbury near Stonehenge produced fifteen antlers placed at the foot and head of the skeleton and at Hunter's Barrow, also in Wiltshire, a cremation was accompanied by the skeleton of a dog and five finely made flint arrowheads surrounded by a wreath of antlers. Again in Wiltshire a pit excavated at Winklebury Camp revealed not only a complete red deer skeleton but also those of twelve foxes, and at that mysterious monument Stonehenge itself, over one hundred antlers have been recovered from the ditch which surrounds the site. Further afield in a tomb excavated on the tiny Holm of Papa Westray North in the Orkneys were more than a dozen pairs of antlers.

The magical power of antlers appears to have been seen by the neolithic peoples as being of some benefit to the dead, as all these examples indicate. A gruesome find from Norton Bavant in Wiltshire gives further evidence of this, for here was discovered a batch of skeletons in disarray of which nearly every skull had been smashed, probably with a flint lump found close by. What was of significance, however, was the fine antler which had been deliberately placed amongst this confusion, as if waiting to reactivate the remains it stood guard over.

Now we visit Grimes Graves, the neolithic flint mines in Norfolk. Covering over 34 acres, the mines consist of 360 shafts, a few of which are open to the public. Red deer antlers were the main tool used in digging the mines, but one shaft was found to hold perhaps England's most significant prehistoric ritual deposit. A shaft had been quarried but had proved to be unproductive. To ensure that future shafts should be more successful, an altar of flints had been built by the miners in front of a ledge upon which was placed a carved chalk figurine in the likeness of an obviously pregnant woman. Antlers were heaped around and on top of the flint pile and next to this array were also found several chalk balls and a chalk phallus. It seems unlikely that the antlers in this configuration were merely examples of the miners' tools, and they appear to have had some religious meaning. The phallus and figurine have obvious fertility aspects, combining to influence the underground chambers to yield more flint. At the neolithic henge of Maumbury Rings near Dorchester another similar find was unearthed, consisting of ritual deposits in the ditch. Here were excavated a number of flint balls and large, chalk phalli, one of which was discovered in close association with two antlered skulls.

The antlers' significance in these two examples is surely connected with the other deposits, the annual growth symbolising fertility and new life. It is probable also that the curvilinear shape of antlers was noticed by our neolithic ancestors to have a resemblance to the shape of a woman, which is of special relevance to the Grimes Graves deposit. Michael Dames has drawn a connection with antlers and the neolithic goddess in her winter or death aspect, based on the finding of roebuck antlers in the West Kennet Long Barrow near Avebury, which he sees as being representative of the great goddess. Further afield in ancient Sumer we find that the goddess of childbirth, Ninharsag, had as her emblem a stag. Thus antlers reflect a syncretism of masculinity and feminity and this androgyny is well illustrated in a painting, dating from the 15c. called the Land of the Hermaphrodites. This, amongst depictions of humans possessing both sexual characteristics, also features a prominent representation of a stag's head. It is not surprising, therefore, that the stag with its elaborate head gear came to play an important part in early religion. Robert Graves felt that the set of antlers found at the neolithic tomb of Newgrange in Ireland were part of the sacred king's headdress and that the stag was the royal beast of the Danaans, the stag being well represented in Irish mythology.

The burial of antlers was not confined to prehistoric times, however, and an interesting survival from the Roman era is worth mentioning. Two sets were discovered at the base of a pit excavated at Wasperton in Warwickshire. They had been carefully positioned in the form of a square at the centre of which it was apparent that a fire had been lit. Under this arrangement was a sandstone block upon which was scrawled the Latin word FELICITER, meaning "for luck". This use of antlers, even though a continuation of an ancient tradition, seems here to have deteriorated into just a good luck charm. Animal deposits under foundations of buildings and land boundaries continued well into historical times and an excavation at Kingston-upon-Thames produced from a 12c. boundary ditch the skulls of a dog and a red deer, again probably placed there to ensure good fortune.

There is one more noteworthy instance of the use of antlers in a ritual setting and that is to be found in a Romano-British temple dating from the fourth century at Brean Down near Weston-super-Mare. It was situated on a peninsula which juts into the sea and was probably cut off from the mainland by marshes. It therefore seems that it would have been necessary to reach it by ferry followed by a steep climb. Adjacent to the main temple was a smaller building which contained a store of antlers. Their presence here indicates a ritual usage continued from the neolithic period and, as such, antlers appear to have retained their potency as symbols, even though the nature of their use here cannot now be ascertained.

The power of the antler seems to have been a recognised phenomenon wherever deer were found and an example from China shows the high regard given them. The Chinese malu deer shed their antlers each winter and they are nearly fully formed again by May, but at this stage

Great Ragg'd Horns

*Chinese antlered head, Zhou Dynasty, 4th - 3rd century B. C.
(British Museum)*

they are not completely hard and still contain blood vessels. Nevertheless it is to obtain these antlers that the malu are hunted, for they are eagerly sought after and exchange hands for large sums. When ground into a powder they are used in various forms of medicinal treatment and are often considered to be a kind of elixir of life. The emperors of ancient China highly prized the use of the powder, which was one of the most treasured ingredients in the apothecary of Chinese healers. It was said by the Tungus tribesmen that an old man should take five grams both at night and in the morning, which would ensure that his circulation would improve and he would generally become more youthful and vigorous. The essence of the antler is thus seen to be a source of growth and renewal in many cultures.

The reindeer hunters of the far north still believe that the mother of the universe took the form of a reindeer doe and their mythology contains legends of pregnant women who are the rulers of the world. These women are portrayed as being hairy all over and bearing antlers on their heads, just like Herne himself. Turning southwards to Bulgaria we find another doe, complete with a set of antlers, in the form of a ritual vase in this shape dating from the sixth millenium B.C. This pottery figure is decorated with crescent moons, thereby revealing the association between the deer and some form of moon worship. The importance of deer is also well attested in Slavic countries and in Hungarian folklore there are stories and songs told about the astral deer. This fabulous animal, which is a messenger from God, carries upon its antlers the sun, the moon and the stars. Russia has a tale of a wondrous stag with a thousand ends to its antlers upon which are a hundred thousand candles which burn without being lit and extinguish themselves.

Which brings us to the most important stag tradition in the British Isles, the "Blowing of the Stag" ceremony at old St. Paul's Cathedral in London. Legend has it that St. Paul's was built on the site of the Temple of Diana by the mythical King Brutus, who gave his name to Britain. In 1830, however, digging work in Foster's Lane northeast of St. Paul's revealed a stone altar dedicated to Diana. Later a bronze statuette of the goddess also turned up at the Deanery of St. Paul's and Blackfriars, southwest of the cathedral. Thus there is some evidence of a Dianic cult in the area, but whether there was a temple at the site it is not possible to say.

What can be said, however, is that up to the 16c. at least a ceremony took place twice a year on the Feast of the Conversion and again on the Feast of the Commemoration of St. Paul. A report from 1598 describes the ceremony, stating that on the first occasion a doe and on the second a buck were given by the keepers and sherriffs of Hertfordshire and Essex to the Dean and Chapter, whose land they had purchased. The ceremony commenced when a keeper, wearing a tunic portraying a stag on its breast would lead the deer up to the high altar. Having been blessed, the deer was then slaughtered, its head cut off and fixed to the top of a pole to be displayed and the body roasted as a feast for all concerned. After this part of the ceremony was completed, a procession led the way out of the cathedral via the west door with the deer's head, complete with antlers in the case of the buck, at the front for all to see. Outside the doors, the keepers would blow long blasts on their horns to the four points of the compass, whilst more hornblowers would do the same throughout the city to announce to the people of London that the ceremony was over.

The stag was sacred to the goddess Diana and that she was associated with the hunt and it is therefore possible that this ancient ceremony may well have originated in pre-Christian Roman times or even before. As already described in this chapter, humankind's fascination with deer and antlers goes back a very long time and this may well have been a very ancient survival in the same vein as the Abbots Bromley Horn Dance (see Chapter 6).

Locally, of course, Berkshire itself has strong connections with deer and Windsor Forest has been the haunt of these animals since time immemorial. One has only to look at the Royal County's emblem a stag and oak tree to realise the importance of deer to the area, no doubt because to hunt these animals was very much a royal pastime. Michael Petry goes further, however, and sees the county's emblem as hearking back to Berkshire's origins when its name (oakgroveshire) was a reference to Windsor itself. His theory was that the area around the

Berkshire antlers - The Horns public house, Crazies Hill

mound upon which the Round Tower stands was an ancient sacred place where an oak cult once existed. This may well have some foundation, for a similar case concerns the Tower of London which was a sacred site during the Celtic period. The mythical Bran is said to have had his head cut off and buried where the Tower now stands and for this reason the modern day Druids have chosen this site for their Spring equinox ceremony. It is very probable therefore that the locality of Windsor Castle was sacred in prehistoric times and may well have been a site which was favoured as a cult centre, perhaps once being the home of shamans bearing antlers upon their heads.

So here we have a long tradition of antlers' attraction to humankind and their qualities seem to symbolise strength, fertility, new life, sexuality and the uniting of the male and female principles. That a figure such as

Inn sign, Herne's Oak public house, Winkfield

Herne should be said to bear a set of these "ragg'd horns" is no surprise since the legend of Herne the Hunter is concerned with death and renewal. Herne is reputed to haunt the area during the winter, and his death and return to life with the magical help of Urswick can be seen to represent the "death" of the natural world during the winter period only to be reborn in the spring. The deer's rutting season in autumn when the stags charge each other, engaging their antlers in battle must have been a prelude to the arrival of the winter's Wild Hunt led by Herne, who has adopted the stag's symbols of power and regeneration in his seasonal race through the forest and countryside of Berkshire.

The Horned One

Depictions of horned deities and other figures bearing either horns or antlers are to be found throughout Europe as well as further afield. The significance of antlers has been explored in the previous chapter and the notion of fusing man with animal in the form of a horned god, or mythical beings such as satyrs, takes us back to the days of our early ancestry when prehistoric tribes would adopt an animal as their totem.

Totemism represents the thought system whereby a tribe associates itself with an animal which becomes their emblem, with the tribe's fortunes and misfortunes being magically bound up with those of the animal in question. Often the tribe would claim descent from some originating "great father (or mother) animal" and would see itself at one with the spirit of that particular creature. In some instances the spirits of man and beast would merge to give rise to mythical creatures such as centaurs, which the Greek myths describe as half man half horse, with a man's upper torso in the place of the horse's head. The horse was in fact the totem animal of a tribe who called themselves the Centaurs and who inhabited Magnesia in northern Greece. The most famous of course was Cheiron, the wise, who acted as fosterfather to the hero Jason.

Many animal species were adopted as totems, various American Indian tribes selecting deer, wolves, bears and buffaloes amongst others, but plants and inanimate objects were also chosen, such as reed grass, water and sand. As well as being considered the tribe's ancestral spirit, individuals were thought to be united with their totem upon death. The animal concerned became taboo, not to be killed or eaten except on very special occasions. Examples of totem animals are thought to have been discovered in the prehistoric tombs of the Orkney Islands. The most famous is one which has become known as the Tomb of the Eagles, constructed by the neolithic people around 3100 B.C. Amongst numerous human bones and skulls were found the carcasses of ten sea-eagles, giving rise to the notion that this bird was the tribe's totem. This is reinforced by finds in other Orkney tombs, which included variously: dog skulls (24 at one), songbirds, foxes, cormorants, thirteen deer skeletons and at one more than a dozen sets of antlers. Thus we can see that totemism is an ancient and important feature of primitive societies and no doubt involved dressing up as the favoured animal or bird, in imitation of the creature and becoming a human animal.

Greek mythology is responsible for giving us the most well known man-beast the Minotaur. It is also the first example we shall meet of a horned figure. The Minotaur, which means "bull of Minos", took the form of a man with a bull's head complete with horns and its slaying by another Greek hero, Theseus, is one of the best known of the classical myths. Minos was the title of a Cretan dynasty which used a bull as its emblem, bulls featuring in many ancient religions, their horns symbolic of strength and power. The Cretan palace of Knossos was adorned with many frescoes, some of which depicted young men and women leaping over bulls. Although the bull cult became predominant on the island, there were also a goat cult and a stag cult, all three representing the veneration of horned beasts.

Another figure bearing horns was the Greek god Pan who, although he was human from the waist up, took the form of a goat lower down as well as bearing goat's horns. He lived in Arcadia, where he watched over flocks and herds and aided hunters in the chase. However, he had a wilder side and was associated with lustful energy and fertility and accompanied the frenzied Maenads in their drunken orgies. He was also leader of the goat spirits or satyrs, who were smaller versions of Pan himself. He gave us the word panic, as it was said that if he was disturbed out in the countryside he would let out a great shout which would cause the perpetrators to Panic. It is perhaps significant that Pan's father was Hermes, whom we shall meet later.

In ancient Egypt, where many gods and goddesses were depicted bearing the heads of animals, the goddess Hathor was portrayed with cow's horns and the god Osiris bore the horns of fertility. Although originally worshipped as a cow, Hathor was later represented as human with the horns upon her head enclosing a disc of the moon. Due to their curvature and similarity to the waxing or waning moon, horns and,

The Horned One

incidentally, horseshoes, were often associated with a moon goddess. In her aspect as guardian of the dead, Hathor was sometimes shown with the setting sun receiving the souls of the dead, which is a theme we shall see repeated when we come to discuss Hermes and the Saxon god Woden (see chapter 5).

Horned humans are not unknown to medical science, since there is a rare skin disease which goes by the name of Cornu Cutaneum. This manifests itself in a cutaneous outgrowth which often resembles a horn since it is mainly found growing from the scalp, one recorded case involving growths one foot long and fourteen inches around the base. There was a famous example named Francois Trovillow, also known as the Horned Man of Mezieres who died in 1698 and another known as the Horned Kaffir of Africa visited London and was apparently still alive in the 1920's.

The widespread appearance of horned figures in many cultures of the world has prompted the author Stan Gooch to suggest a very ancient origin. His view is that the horned figure is a folk memory of neanderthal man, whose thick tufted eyebrows gave the impression of a human being with horns growing out of his head. Thus cromagnon man, our immediate ancestors, upon seeing this unusual kind of human, may well have remained apart from these strange beings and all manner of ideas would have grown up about them including, perhaps, the notion that they were half animal. So the idea of horned figures may go back many thousands of years to the days when there was not one but two varieties of homo sapiens upon this planet.

The neanderthals themselves appear to have had a feeling for horns, as indicated by a burial found in TeshikTash near Samarkand in Uzbekistan. Here the body was found accompanied by five or six pairs of horns belonging to the Siberian mountain goat, which had been arranged upright in pairs, pointed ends down. This is obviously a deposit of a ritual nature and is one of the very earliest of such finds. There is a surviving goat cult today which exists in the Khingove valley in Asia and is derived from the cult of Burkh or mountain goat. The horns of this animal are collected and used as ritual offerings, the people believing this will ensure prosperity.

The idea of the man-beast has not yet died out, as there are still reports to this day of apemen, the best known being the Yeti from Asia and Bigfoot from North America. Dr. Myra Shackley has made a study of the subject and her conclusions suggest that there may still be a species of man as yet unidentified living in wild, inaccessible regions. Indeed she puts forward the theory that remnants of neanderthal man may have survived into the twentieth century. Such survivals into historical times may well help to reinforce Stan Gooch's idea of neanderthals being the source of horned figures and it would indeed be the scientific discovery of the century if live specimens were encountered.

That the beast still lurks within us was one of the themes of H.G. Wells's "theological grotesque" entitled The Island of Dr. Moreau and published in 1896. The novel concerns the attempts by the vivisectionist, Dr. Moreau, to turn animals into human beings, resulting in mutants called the Beast-People. The characters include a Leopard Man, Swine Men, a Bear-Bull, a Hyaena/Swine hybrid as well as a satyrlike creature combining ape and goat. The book highlights the dual nature of humanity, with the beast ever present beneath a civilized exterior. The island on which the action takes place represents human society with all the pain and folly of individual lives, which appear to start from and lead to nowhere. The story expresses the confusion as to mankind's origins which was apparent at the end of the 19c. with the dust still not settled on the revolution instigated by Darwin.

Wild men not far removed from animals were believed to exist in many lands and, indeed, are still believed in today in certain countries. Living a near animal life in woods and forests, they were thought to be strong and agressive with a powerful sexuality and often appeared to be mad. They were frequently depicted in medieval art and literature and, like Wells's Beast-People, they represented the bestiality in humankind, a trait inherited, and never fully sublimated, from his primitive forbears. The Wild Man was traditionally portrayed as hairy and a hunter who ate his prey raw. He has thus close affinities with Herne who, dressed in deerskins, was a hunter and who actually went mad before finally

The Horned One

Cernunnos. Carved stone found under Nôtre Dame, Paris (Service Photographique de la Réunion des Musées Nationaux, France)

committing suicide. We can therefore see a long history of the idea of wild men or man-beasts and Herne certainly reveals aspects of himself which he shares with these creatures.

But we must now return to Herne himself and his antlers, and it is time to narrow the field of study to figures who specifically wear these distinctive horns. Although the horned god is found in many cultures, the antlered god is not so common. The province of Ch'ang-sha in China, however, provides us with a far-flung example. Here was discovered a carved wooden head of a god to which had been attached a pair of antlers, the carving dating from about the fourth or third century B.C. It is not surprising to find such a figure here, however, as we have seen in the previous chapter that the efficacy of antlers was held in high esteem by the Chinese.

Nevertheless, the most well known stag-god comes from much nearer home, being a deity of the pagan Celts who inhabited our islands prior to the arrival of the Romans. His name was Cernunnos, so identified from a stone altar discovered under Notre Dame in Paris, which depicts the head and shoulders of a bearded man who bears a set of antlers upon which are hung two torcs. Above the head appears the name Cernunnos in Roman letters, thus identifying the figure positively, though whether he was known by this name throughout the Celtic world is not known.

In ancient Gaul Cernunnos as a cult figure is well attested, with a number of stone carvings showing a horned figure coming from France as well as elsewhere on the Continent. In fact the Celtic cult probably developed from horned gods worshipped in the bronze age or even earlier, and an example from Denmark illustrates this point. The figure takes the form of a rock carving portraying a horned god who, as well as being naked and phallic, bears a sword and holds a ship in one hand. This linking of phallic, horned figures with ships appears to be common in bronze age Denmark and perhaps it represents the conveying of souls after death in a ship to the Underworld, as Charon ferries the dead across the River Styx in Greek mythology. The theme of guiding the souls of the departed also appears in connection with the Wild Hunt (see chapter 5).

The Horned One

Cernunnos, formerly described as Oceanus. Roman mosaic from Verulamium (St. Albans Museum)

The cult of the horned god came to great prominence in the Celtic period and was overshadowed only by that of the head. It was well established in Britain before the arrival of the Romans and certainly continued through the occupation period. Indeed there is a fine example of a Roman mosaic in the Verulamium Museum at St. Albans which features the head of a god which was formerly identified as Oceanus, a marine deity, because of what were seen as lobster claws growing from his head. But this is now generally believed to be a variant of Cernunnos and the claws are now considered to be antlers. Coming as it does from an important Roman town, i.e. Verulamium, it shows the prevalence of the idea of a horned god in the British Isles.

The horned god was not always represented with stag's antlers, but sometimes with ram's or bull's horns. Nevertheless they are all symbolic of power, vitality and fertility. It is likely that these ideas are behind the rock carving discovered in Val Camonica in Italy which dates to about the fourth century B.C. An antlered figure dressed in what appears to be a long garment stands with a torc on either arm and before him stands a smaller phallic figure. Perhaps this scene represents a god and worshipper and this could well be an early form of Cernunnos, which is reinforced by the nearby picture of a horned serpent, which is generally associated with the god. The snake's habit of sloughing its skin was seen by the Celts as a symbol of renewal and as such was connected with the dying god's resurrection (see Chapter 7 and footnote).

The most well known example of the serpent depicted together with Cernunnos is on the famous Gundestrup cauldron. Found in 1891 at Gundestrup in Jutland, Denmark, it had been purposely dismantled and deposited as a votive offering in about the first century B.C. It is made of silver and both the inner and outer faces are decorated with figures of gods and various cult scenes, and the whole was originally covered with

----

Footnote: Another figure with a name containing the CERN root is that of the Ulster hero Conall Cernach who, in "The Driving of Fraich's Cattle", attacks a castle guarded by a serpent. This may well be a remnant of a snake/horned god association.

a thin layer of gold foil. The scene which concerns us, however, is that showing Cernunnos sitting in a Buddha-like pose with a torc in his right hand and a ram-headed serpent in his left (see footnote). He is surrounded by all manner of animals, but most prominent is the figure of a stag, its antlers almost touching those of the god's. Here Cernunnos appears as "lord of the animals", a trait he shared in common with Hermes who was the guardian of all animals of the land, sea and air and thus presided over things of our earthly realm. This Lord of the Animals figure was considered amongst primitive hunters to be an entity who had power over wild nature and who had to be propitiated to ensure successful hunting. Like Pan and Herne, such figures were often depicted in half-human half-animal guise.

The ram-headed serpent was not uncommonly associated with Cernunnos and was probably linked to the stag-god via the symbolism of the snake. As we have seen, antlers were regarded as symbols of fertility and sexuality and the snake's phallic appearance, especially topped with a ram's head, has obvious sexual overtones. The relevance of the ram's head is almost certainly due to its being that of another horned animal and therefore is in sympathy with the antlered head of the god himself. Now there does not appear to be a direct connection here with Herne, although Ainsworth did feature snakes in his novel when Herne made an appearance. But he was said to wield a chain and it does not require much effort of imagination to see a development from a serpent to a chain .

The serpent was a potent symbol in ancient times and, as with the oak and with antlers, was associated with fertility due to the periodic sloughing of its skin. It was also seen in connection with the sun and its frequent portrayal in an "S" shape provided the link with its similarity to that age-old solar symbol, the swastika. It is not uncommon to find the serpent depicted alongside a sun god. Indeed

---
Footnote: Recent research has suggested that the cauldron's designs originate from eastern Europe and that perhaps the motifs themselves have associations with lands as far away as India.

The Horned One

Antlered god from the Gundestrup cauldron (Nationalmuseet, Denmark)

The Horned One

Figure holding stags from the Gundestrup cauldron (Nationalmuseet, Denmark)

Jupiter was sometimes revered as such, perhaps under Celtic influence, and one statue from Seguret in France shows him standing next to an oak tree entwined by a snake. Here we see a connectedness between the sun, fertility, the oak and the serpent, all aspects included within Herne's story.

Perhaps Herne indeed was originally a variant of Cernunnos and gradually over the centuries his accompanying snake became transformed into a chain. That this form of imagery had evolved and was still extant in the medieval period is shown in a carving to be found

The Devil in chains, a Norse carving from Kirkby Stephen church, Cumbria (By Jessica Lofthouse, from "North Country Folklore", pub. Robert Hale 1976)

at Kirkby Stephen church in Cumbria. Here we find a Viking portrayal of a horned figure bound in chains. It is obviously male and bears a set of ram's horns, but what makes it interesting is that both his arms and legs are bound together with a continuous chain. Thus we have a clear connection of a horned figure and chains. It is also significant that this figure dates from Viking times, for chains feature in rituals in honour of Woden, and Tacitus tells of the Semnones, a Swabian tribe, who would only enter a grove sacred to the god when bound in chains. We shall examine in the next chapter Woden's relationship with Herne and it may not be inappropriate to note that Hermes' wand of office, the caduceus, took the form of two intertwined snakes.

The link between Cernunnos and Hermes is very curious, in that the astrological symbol for Hermes is ☿ which, as John Rowan tells us, incorporates the three horned animals:

Stag's Antlers

Serpent with Ram's Horns

Bull of Earth

Hermes' role was as psychopomp, or guide to the Underworld to the souls of the dead, but he also had a fertility aspect. The god's herms, which were stone pillars placed at special sites such as crossroads throughout the ancient Mediterranean, had two distinctive features, i.e. a head and, halfway down the pillar, a phallus. Thus here again we have connecting ideas - fertility, conducting souls, horns, Hermes, Herne and Cernunnos. These recurring concepts and personnages turn up in different forms in a variety of cultures and what we are seeing are variations on common themes.

In British tradition, the horned god represents the renewal of life and energy at spring time, but furthermore he is also representative of the underworld and thus death and cold. As god of the waxing year or Oak

King he stands for the light half of the year contesting the world with the god of the waning year or Holly King. At midsummer, when the oak tree is in full flower, the tribal oak king was ritually sacrificed, representing the end of his reign, giving rise to the six months' rule of the Holly King. The latter is the Green Knight beheaded in the traditional story, only to rise again unhurt and the two kings symbolically defeat and succeed each other every six months. This theme is repeated in many folk customs such as the Padstow 'Obby 'Oss and in mummers' plays where St. George kills the Turkish knight. The birth-vigour-death-renewal cycle was all important to ancient man, who saw himself as part of the natural world. It is therefore not surprising that an idea so ingrained on the consciousness of early people should reveal itself in so many folk traditions and customs.

Such traditions have their origins in the distant past and it is to prehistory again that we turn for evidence of horned god worship in Britain. The Cornavii or People of the Horn who lived in the area of Caithness in Scotland may well have worshipped a horned god. Ptolemy, the Roman historian, mentions their name in the second century A.D. It is also said that a deer goddess cult existed in the Highlands of Scotland and that the deer has always been regarded there as a supernatural animal. Fairy women were believed to be able to turn themselves into the form of a red deer. Staying with women, there is concrete evidence of a horned goddess cult in the form of a picture from a fragment of pottery. Dating from the second century A.D. the piece comes from Richborough, Kent and shows the bust of a woman bearing horns. Another depiction from France, is in the shape of a small bronze figurine of a squatting goddess with a dish in one hand, a cornucopia in the other and a set of antlers sprouting from her head. Generally, the horned deity is male and these female examples are the exception, but they were important enough to have left a memory in an Irish folktale. Part of the tale consists of horned, supernatural women who carry out the spinning and weaving for a lazy wife.

As to other examples of Cernunnos figures in Britain, one stands out and was recently found at Peterfield in Hampshire. It takes the form of a silver coin depicting the only known certain image of a deity dating from the British Celtic period. Dating from around 20 A.D. it features the head of a bearded and moustached god with antlers, between which sits a crown surmounted by a sunwheel.   Here, then, we see the association of antlers, the sun and a deity indicating the concepts of growth and fertility. Another example emanates from Cirencester, the Roman town of Corinium. It portrays the antlered god in the normal squatting position and on either side of his antlers are purses full of coins or possibly cornucopias full of grapes, either way indicating a god of fertility and plenty. Ram-headed serpents are also portrayed, taking the place of the god's legs. We have already noted the association of the serpent with Cernunnos and it is perhaps appropriate here to note the god's "twinning" with the Roman god of war, Mars, for he too was displayed in the company of a serpent. During the Roman occupation of Britain it was the custom of the invaders to link their own gods to what they considered the native equivalent. The most famous is the goddess Sul-Minerva, worshipped at the great spa of Aquae Sulis at Bath. Another Roman god, this time Jupiter, has been associated with the antlered god in the form of a dedication where the name Cernenus, presumably a variant of Cernunnos, appears with Jupiter, the thunder god. The Celts had their own thunder god, Taranis, and it therefore seems strange for Cernunnos to be linked with Jupiter rather than Taranis. However, Celtic religion was not rigid and it could well be that a local Cernunnos cult had thunder aspects, which may have relevance when considering Herne and his oak, the thunder tree.

Turning from Celtic to Classical mythology, one story of special significance is that of the myth of Actaeon. This unfortunate young man had the misfortune to spy the goddess Artemis bathing in a stream, whereupon he stopped to watch her. However Artemis spotted him and to prevent him bragging to his friends about seeing her nakedness she immediately transformed him into a stag which was then torn to pieces by Actaeon's own hounds. There is a fine mosaic from Cirencester portraying an antlered Actaeon with his hounds attacking him. Robert Graves sees Actaeon as the sacred king of a stag cult who was sacrificed at the end of his reign of half a Great Year or fifty months, his co-king reigning for the second fifty months. This is, of course, reminiscent of the eternal struggle of the Oak King and Holly King.

Plutarch records that as late as the first century A.D. a man who had been dressed up in stag's skins was still hunted and killed on Mount Lycaeum in Arcadia. The ancient Greeks provided us with many mythical stories and Artemis was one of the most popular goddesses. She was Lady of the Wild Things and protector of animals and she was also fond of the hunt and especially loved hunting stags. Known by the Romans as Diana, she had much in common with Herne the Hunter. Perhaps she too was once worshipped as a stag-goddess in earlier times.

The horned god, then, is not only widespread and of ancient origin but is specially prominent in western Europe and Britain. It is likely that he is the Dis Pater, or Father of the Gods, whom Julius Caesar identified as the ancestor of all the Gauls. In particular, the stag-god was singularly revered, especially in the company of the ram-headed serpent. The horned god appears to have made a deep impression on early peoples such as the Celts and perhaps Herne the Hunter is an example of this veneration which, rather than die out completely, has been kept alive in the form of a folk tale. Bob Stewart has commented that the horned god is also the Hunter, the Keeper of the Gateways and the Guardian of the Underworld and, as such, is part of the Goddess's realm. The association of the antlers with the female has already been noted.

However the finer points of the cult of the horned god were to be lost with the arrival of Christianity who transformed the figure into that of the Devil, that horned figure with bestial overtones. It is interesting to note that Ireland's hero, Conall Cernach, is sometimes referred to as the Devil. Thus the sign of the horns became associated with evil and it was naturally assumed that witches worshipped a horned figure as they were deemed to be in league with Satan. It has been claimed that those who attended witches' sabbaths made use of animal masks and no doubt horns would feature in such contexts. It then became the norm for all two-pronged objects to be associated with evil, for they represented the splitting of unity or God into two to create an anti-God. Nevertheless the potency of the horned one was not ignored by Christians, for a religious festival in Brittany commemorates St. Cornely, the patron saint of horned animals and where else should we expect to find such a saint than in a Celtic country?

So how far can we identify Herne with Cernunnos? Of course the similarity of the name is a strong indicator and, even though Herne has been overlaid with romantic embellishments, there does seem to be a probability that elements of the horned god have formed a base for Herne and his story. Apart from the obvious antlers, the possibility that the chain may once have been the ram-headed serpent is supportive evidence. Herne's appearance around the winter solstice also reveals him to have connections with fertility, the regenerative god appearing amongst the season of death and cold to banish them and ultimately bring back fecundity in the spring and summer. It can never be said, of course, that Herne = Cernunnos, since the web of British mythology and folklore cannot be analysed into simple boxes saying x = y. But the complex relationships of the multifarious themes within myths and legends from whatever culture or source is a subject which can provide clues and hints and is itself a rich source of study. What can be said, however, is that Herne's story is set within a land which once revered the horned god to a considerable extent, this continuing well into Roman times. Perhaps it is not unreasonable to postulate vestiges surviving the coming of the Saxons and the merging of them with facets of Woden, who is discussed in the next chapter.

The Devilish Chase

The fact that Herne was a hunter who originally appeared at midwinter confirms that his legend is, in part, a variant of the wider tradition termed the Wild Hunt. Common to most north European cultures, with parallels elsewhere in the world, Wild Hunt stories tell of a spectral hunt which courses across country, through forest or across the sky, usually led by some form of demonic personage with an entourage of ghostly horses, hounds, devils and otherworldly beings. Accompanying the Hunt are all manner of unfortunates. These include unbaptized children, suicides, murderers, adulterers, criminals, blasphemers, witches and freemasons, as well as soldiers, churchmen and courtesans. They are often deformed, with their heads in their chests or facing backwards, or instead have deer's heads in the place of a human's. Others are maimed, with missing heads, limbs or eyes and some even have their entrails hanging out.

Variations of the Wild Hunt are found throughout Europe and the British Isles, and Herne's role is assumed by a variety of other characters according to the locality of the story. In France and Germany he is Charlemagne or Frederick the Great, and in Jutland there is even a Horn the Hunter. In Wales he becomes Gwynn ap Nudd, Lord of the Dead, who inhabited the Celtic underworld Annwn, said, according to one legend, to be situated beneath Glastonbury Tor, and it was to here that he summoned the souls of the departed during his celestial flights. He is associated with another Welsh god of the underworld named Arawn, described in legend as a hunter who pursues a white stag in the company of a pack of hounds called the Cwn Annwn or Hounds of Hell. White, with ears tipped red, they were regarded as harbingers of death. In British mythology these hounds are also known as Yeth Hounds, Yell Hounds, Wish Hounds, Gabriel Hounds, Rachet Hounds, Gabriel Ratchets and variations on these and they were thought to be the souls of unbaptised children who flitted between heaven and earth. The yelping sounds of these so-called hounds were probably the noise made by migrating barnacle geese as they flew overhead by night. Gabriel was the name given to the Hebrew angel who acted as psychopomp, or conductor of souls to heaven, and as such is similar to Hermes who guided souls to the Greek underworld.

The Devilish Chase

Herne the Hunters Wild Hunt by George Cruickshank

Other hunt leaders include Arthur himself, who has a whole body of myth and legend attached to him, with many ancient sites throughout the length and breadth of Britain bearing his name. Indeed there is one specific spot where he is said to actually appear, and that is South Cadbury in Somerset. Famed for being the possible site of the legendary Camelot, South Cadbury hillfort is traditionally held by locals to contain a cavern wherein Arthur lies sleeping. At midnight on midsummer's day he is reputed to ride with his knights over the fort and down to a spring to quench the horses' thirst. There is also an ancient track nearby called Arthur's Lane or Hunting Causeway where sounds of the hunt are heard during the winter months. Like Herne at Windsor this is an instance of a particular figure leading the Wild Hunt at a specific site, and we shall come across others as we continue our search.

A historical personage reputed to lead the Hunt is a character named Wild Edric, who held lands in the Welsh Marches in the 11c. In 1067 he led an uprising against the Normans and in 1069 sacked Shrewsbury. It appears that he was never defeated in battle and eluded capture altogether; in fact he made peace with William the Conqueror and actually joined his side. His death is not recorded and tradition has it that he did not die at all, but had to suffer eternal punishment for changing sides by leading a Wild Hunt. It is said that, along with his fairy wife Godda and his band of followers, he races across country in a furious ride.

He always faces in the direction of the country with which England will be at war in the near future. His troop was seen just before the Crimean War in 1854 galloping past Minsterley in Shropshire. He was seen by a lead-miner and his daughter, the latter disobeying her father's instruction to cover her face or she would go mad. She looked through her spread fingers to see Wild Edric as a dark man with flashing black eyes and curly black hair. He wore a short green coat and cloak and a green cap with a feather in it. He also had a short sword and a horn. Ainsworth gives Herne a horn and it seems that all Wild Huntsmen blow a horn to herald their arrival. Wild Edric was also sighted before the two world wars. In the summer of 1914 he appeared riding eastwards and again in the summer of 1939 he was seen along with Godda. His warnings of war are similar to those Herne is reputed to give at the time of national disaster, a topic which will be covered in chapter 8.

The Devilish Chase

Herne's Wild Hunt

The Devilish Chase

Another huntsman takes the form of the mythical King Herla, said to be one of the early British kings and after whom the Wild Hunt is sometimes named in the form of the Herlathing. Herla and his troops used to wander the countryside in a never-ending march and there is a record of a sighting one midday in 1154 in the Welsh Marches. Apparently they were seen with horses, hounds, hawks and wagons and when they were first sighted the local populace shouted and blew horns, whereupon the whole troop flew up into the air and vanished.

There has been a suggestion of a close connection between Herne and Herla by the similarity of their names. There may be a germ of truth here, but there is another link which is more interesting in that it is relevant to perhaps the most important leader of the Wild Hunt, the Anglo-Saxon god Woden. He was also known as Herian, which later became Herleke and was translated into Latin to give Herlekinus. This again gave the French name Harlequin, and the Wild Hunt in France went under the name, amongst others, of La Mesnie Herlequin. The Harlequin which has survived as a figure into modern times at the festival of Carnival can be traced back to Herla. His costume as it appeared in the 17c. consisted of rags sewn together at random, which harked back to the rough garb of the Wild Huntsman himself. In some parts of France, however, St. Hubert has taken Harlequin's place and at harvest time and on St. Hubert's feast day the saint and his Wild Hunt are said to be heard. Nevertheless, in pre-Christian times there is no doubt that Herian or Woden was to feature as an important figure in Wild Hunt legend. His name is found in folk traditions in mainland Europe and the Wild Hunt is led by him in Holland (Woedende Jager) and Denmark (Odinsjagt).

Woden was essentially a storm god manifesting himself in thunderous movement in the heavens. One of his nicknames was Atridr, which means Rider and reveals him as the horseman who gallops across the sky on his steed, which in Woden's case is his eight-legged horse Sleipnir. He was a major deity both on the Continent and in Anglo-Saxon England. Wednesday derives its name from that of the god - Woden's day - and the Dark Age earthwork of Somerset and Wiltshire - Wansdyke - built to contain the Saxons in the east means "Woden's Ditch". A few place-names also originate from his name, including Woodnesborough in Kent (hill sacred to Woden) and Wednesbury in Staffordshire (Woden's fort).

The Devilish Chase

Returning to Berkshire, there is a possible reference to a Woden's Oak near Chieveley and this interpretation is reinforced by the fact that a host path is recorded nearby and we have seen that Woden was, as Herian, a leader of the host. Woden was also known as Grimnir, which means the masked or hooded one. It was in this form that he appears in a number of Berkshire earthworks, including Grim's Ditches at Aldworth, Grimsbury Castle near Hermitage and Grim's Bank near Padworth. It is interesting to note that references to Woden and trees occur at the aforementioned Chieveley, at a Woden's Oak in Worcestershire and also in some placenames in Scandinavia such as Odenslunda (Woden's Grove) in Scania and Onsved (Woden's Wood) in Zealand. It is therefore apparent that Woden was associated with a tree cult, which ties in well with his, and Herne's, hanging on a sacred tree (see chapter 7). Another connection with the Herne legend is the fact that Woden was sometimes known as the stag or elk and this may well be significant when considering his role as leader of the Wild Hunt at Windsor.

Woden was the chief deity in Anglo-Saxon England, as placename evidence corroborates, and all the early dynasties claimed to be directly descended from the god. Even in the Christian period the Anglo-Saxon royal houses traced their ancestry back to Woden. He was obviously very much revered in those days and must have made a deep impression on his worshippers and was not entirely forgotten by their descendants.

Folk memories of Woden continued up until the last century, as this Lincolnshire remedy for the cure of a fever reveals. An old woman, anxious to cure her grandchild, nailed three horseshoes upon a footboard. As she tapped each shoe with a hammer, she chanted :

> "Father, Son and Holy Ghost,
> Nail the devil to this post
> With this mell I thrice do knock,
> One for God, and one for Wod, and one for Lok."

The god's name itself derives from an old Germanic root meaning furious, wild or mad and is appropriate for a figure who led his troops of dead warriors across the sky to Valhalla, where they engaged in eternal feasting and battling. It was in this respect that Woden earned another nickname,

Valfodr, meaning Father of the Slain. During the autumn and winter period Woden's worshippers, upon hearing the wind tearing through the forest, would say that the god was out riding with his band. They also had a custom whereby they would leave the last sheaf of corn in the field to feed Sleipnir. Herne was said to have gone mad before he committed suicide and coupled with the wild nature of his hunts, there is more than a touch of similarity between him and the wildness of Woden.

The passing overhead of Woden's Hunt was regarded as a portent of some disaster, as were many celestial events such as comets and eclipses. It was also believed that anyone who was unfortunate enough to see the Wild Hunt was likely to be carried off with them, cast to the ground or be made blind or insane and, even worse, to speak to the Wild Huntsman himself meant certain death. The Huntsman was also known to throw down human flesh or even dead infants upon the unfortunate person unlucky enough to see him. Thus here we see a parallel with the tradition of Herne, for it is said that a sighting of him heralds some national disaster and his taking of the cattle and making milk-cows yield blood tell of the fear that he, like Woden, instilled into people.

Other Wild Hunt traditions also involve cattle and a legend from Switzerland tells of the Wild Huntsman lifting cows up into the air. They are either never seen again or reappear three days later milked and only barely alive. In Jutland, Denmark, he is said to tear bulls to pieces as food for his hounds and in Swabia he swoops down to take with him the carcasses of cows which had panicked before slaughter. In Oldenburg farmers whose herds were worried by the Huntsman's hounds left their fattest cow in a field ready for him to take on Christmas Eve. This is not the only superstition concerning cows, Christmas and the Wild Huntsman, however, and an old belief from Berkshire is worth recalling. It appears that at midnight on Christmas Eve all the cattle stand up and low. We shall see further Christmas connections with Herne later in this chapter.

It is also recorded folk custom that if the Wild Hunt was hailed in good cheer, then the hailer would be rewarded. As the Hunt went by a horse's leg would be thrown down and, if kept to the next day, it would turn into a nugget of gold. One is also immune from misfortune if one sees the Hunt whilst riding a horse shod with iron horseshoes. An efficacious

The Devilish Chase

method of keeping the Wild Hunt at bay was to fix a pair of antlers or horns to the gables of one's house. If asked for salt or parsley, the Huntsman will gallop off without causing any harm, and other protections include standing on a white cloth, praying or holding a sprig of hazel, hawthorn or marjoram. Crossroads also negate the power of the Hunt. Not everyone has the ability to see the Wild Hunt, however, but there is a tradition that children born at midnight have the privilege of seeing not only ghosts but also the Wild Hunt. Other persons have automatic immunity, however, and include good churchmen and honest herdsmen. There are even remedies for any misfortune which befalls anybody affected adversely such as waiting one year when, on the Hunt's return, the evil will be undone.

As Christianity took its hold upon the population of Britain, the pagan gods such as Woden lost their influence and were largely forgotten except as figures in folk tales. And so Woden lost his role as Wild Huntsman and other characters took his place, most commonly the Devil, who also bore horns. Other outlandish characters have also taken on the role and it is perhaps appropriate to quote a few instances to see the similarity of these tales to that of Herne and to put him in the context of a tradition which forms a part of wider folk beliefs. To begin down in the south west, the Devil leads the Hunt in this story told in 1921 but which dates back much further. Once there lived at Launceston in Cornwall a good-for-nothing who, whilst crossing Yealm Bridge on the Cornish/Devon border one night, came upon the Devil and his hounds out hunting. The Devil saw him and warned him that if he ever again crossed the bridge by night and interfered with the Hunt, he would die. Although the man was ridiculed, he was known to make long detours to avoid crossing the bridge after the hours of daylight. However, one night he found himself about fifteen miles from home and managed to get a lift on an empty carriage, but when it arrived at Launceston the driver found that his passenger had disappeared. He was subsequently found dead at Yealm Bridge and, as there was no sign of injury, some said it was the work of the Devil, but a verdict of death from natural causes was passed. Another tale from Cornwall tells of an infamous character named Lord Tregeagle. He apparently murdered his wife and children and then went on to marry a number of rich women, whom he also killed, one after the other, for their money. As well as committing other heinous crimes, he condemned himself forever by selling his soul to the Devil. And so it is said that his soul is eternally doomed to wander, and his anguished cry is heard at the height of a storm, as it rages across the Cornish landscape.

Moving to the adjacent county of Devon, we hear of a farmer returning from Widecombe Fair. As he ascended a hill he reached a stone circle, when all of sudden he heard the sound of a hunting horn and baying hounds. Then a rider dressed in black and mounted on a black horse rushed passed him accompanied by a pack of hounds. The farmer, emboldened by drink, called out "Hallow Old Nick! Show us some of your game!" at which the rider threw him something which he caught. After the Wild Hunt had disappeared into the night, the farmer found that he was holding the dead body of his own baby. He galloped home only to find his wife in a distressed state saying that their baby had disappeared from its cot. The farmer then told his wife what had happened to him and showed her the still body of their deceased child.

Remaining in Devon we visit the Dewerstone, a rocky crag named after Dewer known as the Wish Huntsman. He is reported to terrorise Dartmoor at night in the company of his Wish Hounds and he appears at the top of the Dewerstone as a figure dressed in black who holds a whip whilst at the bottom sits a huge black dog. The tradition is that the Hunt, led by Dewer, would chase unfortunate souls up to the top of the highest crag and then vanish, leaving them to fall over the edge to their deaths. Also said to lead the Wish Hounds across Dartmoor is none other than Sir Francis Drake, who apparently was known to have an interest in the occult. He is reputed, on stormy and moonless nights, to drive a black coach drawn by headless horses.

Further north into Somerset, the locals who live on the Quantock Hills avoid going out on stormy nights near the Triscombe Stone, since it is then that the hounds are likely to be heard running. It has been known for the phantom pack to leave their normal haunt of the hills and there was once a report of a dark huntsman being seen waiting beneath some trees in a lane near the village of Combwich. The following day the local witch was found dead and it was said that the Devil had come to take his own. This is another example of the Wild Huntsman claiming another soul and this collecting of souls is a common theme with the Wild Hunt,

The Devilish Chase

be it the Devil, Woden or Herne with his band of forest keepers.

The capture of a soul is well illustrated by another tale from Somerset, this time from Crowcombe, to where an old woman was wending her way to market with her pony carrying her wares. Unfortunately, instead of setting out early in the morning, on this occasion she mistook the time and she left before midnight. After a while she fell asleep on the pony and when she awoke, she found the animal trembling with fear in a field. Then she saw a white rabbit hopping past her terrified and it was then she heard the baying hounds. She felt sorry for the rabbit and let it hop into her pannier. However, the pony wouldn't move and she then heard the sound of approaching hooves and a black rider came towards her and stopped. The rider's horse had horns which shone with a green light and the hounds breathed green fire. The black rider asked the old woman if she had seen a rabbit pass by and when she shook her head he led his hunt off into the night. The pony then decided to move and galloped until they reached a ford, whereupon the old woman opened her pannier. But it was no rabbit that emerged but a beautiful lady, who thanked the old woman for saving her. Apparently she had been a witch when young and when she died she was condemned to be hunted by the Devil and his Yeth Hounds, until she could get behind them, which the old woman had enabled her to do. At which she disappeared.

This last story is of interest in that the horse had horns and this is one of the few instances, apart from Herne, that features horns or antlers in connection with the Wild Hunt. Another takes the form of the aforementioned folk belief which maintains that to attach horns or antlers to the outside of a house is a protection against a visit from the Wild Huntsman. It is also said that whoever sticks his head out of a window to see the Wild Hunt will sprout antlers, just like Herne. It is therefore probable that an antlered figure was once a feature of the Wild Hunt throughout Britain, surviving only in the legend of Herne the Hunter at Windsor.

The hounds breathing fire is an example of the weird companions with which the Wild Huntsman rides, other types being headless horses or dogs with red eyes. Spectral dogs are not uncommon in British folklore, perhaps the best known being Black Shuck who haunts East Anglia. He again may be headless or at other times have only one eye or two which glow red in the dark. A local example concerns the White Dog of Feens, which appears in a wood at Littlewick Green near Maidenhead in Berkshire. Whenever this spectral hound is heard howling, it is said to herald the appearance of a ghostly hunt which is accompanied by a pale young lady dressed in grey named Dorcas Noble. She appears to have been a witch, since it is said that she made use of sorcery in order to win back the affections of her lover whom she had lost to another. A further example of a lost soul claimed by the demon hunter. However, such hounds appear mainly in the east and north of England and it could be that they are a memory from Viking times of the Hounds of Woden, the god's wardogs, which took the form of two wolves named Geri and Freki. Herne himself is said to be accompanied by two hounds and considering his connections with Woden it is not fanciful to see them as descendants of those hounds which accompanied the god. Like his dogs, the Huntsman's horse often has red eyes and breathes flame. It is sometimes deformed, perhaps being headless or twolegged and it leaves no hoofprints in the snow and it cannot be shot.

On the Continent it is also known for the horse to be replaced by a dog or even a fiery goat. Staying across the Channel, we come across a German variant of the Wild Hunt, involving a baron who lived in the castle of Rodenstein in the Oderwald. This baron was of a wild and lawless disposition and one Sunday morning found him out hunting. To summon the hunt and hounds he blew a loud blast on his horn and at this two strangers dressed for the hunt rode up on either side of him. On his right was a young, fairhaired man of pleasant countenance mounted on a white horse and on his left the rider was swarthy and savage looking and he rode a jet black horse. The hunt then commenced and soon a stag was being pursued, which ran off into a field of ripening corn. The farmer and colleagues prayed that the hunt would not follow and the fair rider appeared to agree as he hesitated to continue, but the dark rider urged the hunt on and the corn was trampled to dust, to the peasants' distress. The chase carried on until it came across a man tending a herd of cows, which the hounds furiously attacked. The herdsman pleaded with the baron to call them off and the two strangers urged him two ways, the fair one to hold off and the swarthy one to carry on. The baron took the latter's advice and all the cattle as well as the herdsman were killed. The hunt

The Devilish Chase

continued and came to a wood within which lived a hermit. This pious man was appalled by the violence of the chase and tried reasoning with the baron who, again, took the advice of the evil rider and raised his whip to strike the unfortunate hermit. But at that instant a change came over him and his horse became a demon steed and the baron became doomed to ride the hunt until the end of time. With his hounds running with him, he hunts a phantom stag and is pursued by avenging devils. As with other Wild Hunts, and Herne, his appearance is seen as a portent of some catastrophe.

An unusual example, involving a Wild Huntress, also originates in Germany, this time in the Black Forest. She is reputedly the ghost of the Countess of Elverstein, who had a dispute with her neighbour, the Count of Wurtenberg, about a claim to a piece of land. She apparently laid claim, unlawfully, to a section of forest owned by the count which she wished to hunt. She agreed to meet him in that part of the forest to discuss the matter, but the argument did not go in her favour. However, she swore that she was standing on her own land, which was in fact true since she had filled her shoes with earth from her own property. She added that no power in Heaven or Hell could prevent her from hunting in that part of the forest, for ever if she wished. This was taken at her word, for her punishment was to hunt till the end of time on a demon steed accompanied by a demon pack of hounds.

Female huntresses, although not common, are found elsewhere in myth and legend. In Irish mythology we come across the giantess named Garbh Ogh, who was wont to hunt mountain deer. Accompanied by a pack of seventy hounds with the names of birds, she rode in a chariot drawn by elks and lived off deer's milk and eagles' breasts. The Greek goddess Hecate was also known as a leader of the hunt and she was sometimes portrayed as a whelping bitch. The most well known, however, is the Greek goddess Artemis or Diana of the Romans. Twin sister of Apollo, the sun god, she was the moon goddess who travelled across the night sky in her chariot drawn by four stags with golden antlers. It was her custom to hunt amongst the Arcadian mountains in the company of her nymphs and, in this guise, was regarded as goddess of the chase. Homer referred to her as Agrotera or "She of the Wild Beasts", and she was associated with a stag.

Artemis is also connected with another hunter from the Greek myths, Orion. A giant, he emanated from Boeotia and was considered to be the most handsome man in the world. After he had met up with Artemis, the two of them shared the hunt together. It was then that Artemis' brother, Apollo, became angry at their association and tricked her into killing Orion, who was then placed amongst the stars and the constellation of Orion is one of the best known in the night sky, with his prominent belt made up of three bright stars. Seen best during the autumn and winter, Orion presages rain and storms and is thus akin to Herne in his midwinter appearances. Allied to this is the zodiacal sign of Sagittarius, the archer/hunter and Centaur, whose period covers the winter months of November/December, further confirmation of the association of midwinter and the hunt.

A German tradition from Mecklenburg also involves a female huntress in the form of Frau Gode or Wode. She rode a white horse and her companions were the usual pack of hounds as well as many types of wild animal. Unusually, her appearance was said to bring not disaster but prosperity and she appears to have been a sort of northern Artemis. Staying with the Germanic peoples, the Norse god Uller, who often led the Wild Hunt in the absence of Woden, was associated with winter and thus again is linked with the times of Herne's appearances.

Irmin, the continental Saxon god, has affinities with Orion via his celestial connections in that he would drive his chariot along the Milky Way, which was called Irmin's Way by his worshippers. Irmin is one of a class of figures who, although not leading a Wild Hunt, was reputed to appear along with spectral accompaniment in the night sky, often at winter time. Another such example is that of the Wandering Jew. The legend goes that when Christ, during his agony, requested that he quench his thirst at a horse trough, the Jew whom he asked refused and pointed to a hoof print on the ground which had become full of water and said that he might drink there. From then on the Wandering Jew was condemned to drive a team of horses whenever a storm was raging, only to be released from this task come Judgement Day. Remaining on a Biblical theme, during the middle ages the Wild Hunt was known as Cain's Hunt or Herod's Hunt, these characters no doubt being thought apt leaders, as murderers, of a band of lost souls.

The Devilish Chase

Souls were also the responsibility of the Valkyries in Germanic mythology. Their task was to select the souls of those killed in battle and, mounted on swift, white horses, to guide them to Valhalla, the realm of Woden. This searching for lost souls is a common idea throughout the world. A further example comes from North America, where the Inuit Indians of Hudson Bay tell of their sightings of the lantern lights held by demons who are wandering through the universe seeking out lost souls. This is a theme common also to Herne and his band of foresters, souls doomed to ride with him to pay for the wrong they did him. It is of interest to note here that there is an ancient belief on the Continent that the souls of the dead were ferried across the Channel to Britain; in fact in north Germany the Wild Hunt is known as the English Hunt.

There have been several historic reports of the Wild Hunt, and one from the year 1091 is worthy of note. It appears that in January of that year a priest from Bonneval near Chartres was on his way to visit a sick person, but on the way had the misfortune to have a close encounter with the Wild Hunt. His report spoke of an endless procession of wretched, tormented souls, including clerics as well as lay men and women and the whole was led by a giant wielding a huge club which he pointed at the priest to order him to stand still as they passed by.

Another sighting of the Wild Hunt happened at Peterborough in 1127. In that year Henry I granted the abbacy of Peterborough to one Henry of Poitou, which was an appointment unpopular with the local people. Immediately after his arrival it was reported by many that they had both heard and seen huge, swarthy huntsmen riding on black horses and goats. Their hounds were jet black and had horrible saucerlike eyes. They were observed in the local parklands and woods and the monks heard their horses throughout the night, and all this carried on from Henry's arrival in February up to Easter. The following century saw a further sighting, for in 1283 the Bishop of Elect of Durham, Anthony Bek, encountered a cousin of Herne called the Gros Veneur, or Great Hunter, whilst hunting in the Forest of Galtres north of York. Whether religious individuals are more prone to encounters with the Wild Hunt is a point to ponder!

A man of the cloth who had many encounters with the supernatural was

The Devilish Chase

Dom Robert Petitpierre, a monk from Nashdom Abbey in Burnham, Buckinghamshire. As an exorcist, he was called to investigate ghostly hauntings and apparitions of all kinds, and one in particular he tells of is relevant to the Wild Hunt. It concerns the owner of a large house who asked an architect friend to add a billiards room by way of an extension to the house. After being built for two or three months, the owner invited the architect round to visit and, during the evening, they duly retired to the new billiards room. However, just as the visitor was about to play a stroke, he looked up in amazement. What he saw charging across the room and right through the billiards table was a ghostly stag followed by a pack of hounds, a hunt and then a monk mounted on a horse. The owner informed him that it had happened every night there was a full moon since the room was built. It was therefore decided to raise the floor eighteen inches so that the spectral hunt would appear out of sight, but apparently this was not sufficient and subsequently only the heads of the apparitions rushed through the table. The solution turned out to be not to play billiards on the night of the full moon! All in all a fascinating account, which dates from the 1920's and was situated in the Thames Valley, although how near to Windsor is not known. The connection with the moon is unusual in tales of the Wild Hunt for, as we have seen, they are normally associated with midwinter.

Which brings us to an unexpected relation of Herne, also with antler connections and midwinter visits - Father Christmas or Santa Claus. Although the figure as we know him today derives largely from the nineteenth century, his origins go back much further and have much in common with Herne the Hunter.

The people of Lappland and Siberia consist of various tribes, often known as the reindeer people, whose culture and customs date back many hundreds, perhaps thousands, of years. The reindeer has always been, like the buffalo to the American Indians, the source of nearly all their needs, providing them with not only food and clothing, but also utensils and ornaments. Their importance extended into the realms of religion and mythology and every reindeer was believed to be a personification of the Reindeer Spirit, which was a kind of spiritual guardian of the tribe or totem. In times of trouble or whenever some kind of communication was required with this Spirit, then the tribal shaman was consulted to act as

87

The Devilish Chase

A Tungus shaman

"interpreter" of the Spirit's "word".

The shaman is responsible for the welfare of the tribe, as both medical and spiritual healer, and via ecstatic trances is able to enter the upper or lower worlds inaccessible to ordinary mortals, including the realm inhabited by the Reindeer Spirit. This supernatural animal, a symbol of the origins of the tribe which traced its origins back to it, would impart its benificence to the tribe via the shaman who then passed it on to the tribespeople. This the shaman would do by visiting people's houses, and in Siberia winter dwellings are built of logs supported above a hole in the ground with a smokehole in the roof directly above the fire. This hole, incidentally, is also the main entrance and exit to the dwelling. Thus we have two of the elements to the Santa Claus story the bearer of gifts (from the gods) entering the house during the wintertime via the chimney.

It is pertinent to note that these shamans made use of the hallucinogenic mushroom the fly agaric to help induce the trance state, during which they would feel the experience of flying, no doubt to the heavenly realms. The reindeer themselves were very partial to this mushroom, which is bright red with white spots, and here again we have two more elements from the Santa Claus story - the colour of Santa's clothes and his flying through the air pulled by a team of reindeer. There are in fact drawings of shamans of the Tungus people of Siberia dressed in reindeer skins, complete with antlers on their heads, Asian versions of Herne the Hunter himself.

It appears that this northern tradition is the origin of Father Christmas, but it must also be added that Woden was also known as a bringer of good things during the winter period, when he was known as the Yuledemon, although he could just as easily bring bad tidings, as his role as Wild Huntsman testifies. In Scandinavian countries, the Julebuck was a figure which appeared wearing a devilish mask and bearing horns and, despite his appearance, brought gifts for children. So here we have some common elements with Herne the Hunter, the antlered deer and the spectral appearances during the winter season. Perhaps all this indicates an origin for Herne way back in the mists of time, since the shamanistic tribes and their tradition may well date back to the last ice age 10,000 years ago.

There also appears to be a connection between the Wild Hunt and the trooping fairies of Ireland. Fairy paths were mentioned in chapter one and tradition has it that Irish fairies would move at various times of the year, often at midwinter. Whilst on the move they were liable to harm or cause illness to those who saw them, and were even known to abduct humans. If a house stood on a fairy path, then the fairies would manifest themselves as a poltergeist and in summer they took the form of whirlwinds. It seems, therefore, that trooping fairies and the Wild Hunt are relics of an idea which dates far back into prehistory.

Thus the Wild Hunt has been around for a long time and, strangely, resurfaced in 1939 in the guise of a country and western song "Riders in the Sky", subsequently turned into an instrumental pop record by the Ramrods in 1961. The ghost rider here drives a "devil's herd" of cattle whose "brands wuz still on fire" and who is fated to round them up

The Devilish Chase

"across these endless skies" for all eternity. The Wild Hunt seems to touch a chord in the human psyche and Windsor's Herne appears to be a localised example of a theme which has meant much to a variety of peoples worldwide.

Another, more serious, example of the theme in the twentieth century comes from the great psychologist Carl Jung. A natural psychic, Jung had vivid dreams and one in particular is relevant here. It appears that on the night before his mother's death he dreamt that he was in a dark jungle with huge boulders, a "primeval landscape" as he described it. All at once he heard a piercing whistle which terrified him, but not so much as what appeared next. A gigantic wolfhound burst through the undergrowth with its jaws open and rushed past him. Jung knew instantly that it had been sent by the Wild Huntsman to take away a human soul.

Jung woke up in terror and the next morning learned the news of his mother's death. He thought that superficially the dream had meant that the Devil had come and taken her away, but a deeper interpretation gave the role to the Wild Huntsman. In his guise of Woden, he had taken Jung's mother to her ancestors, "into that greater territory of the self which lies beyond the segment of Christian morality, taken into that wholeness of nature and spirit in which conflicts and contradictions are resolved".

Herne the Hunter as Wild Huntsman is therefore a primeval symbol dating back to the old stone age when life was harsher and depended on the success of the hunt. This would have special significance during the winter period when food was scarce and it is perhaps the wild, urgent chase which proved necessary at this time of year which ingrained itself into folk memory. That appears to be the reason why Woden, Santa Claus and Herne are all associated with midwinter. The uncertainty of obtaining food and of survival itself manifests itself in bringing of either good or bad tidings from Woden, the gifts from Santa Claus and the warnings of national disaster from Herne. These legendary figures are joined by a host of other persons who also lead the hunt, the Devil being favourite in many instances, but recent centuries bringing with them localised figures of whom Herne is an example. His role as Wild Huntsman places him in a broader context and the parallels described in this chapter reveal the extent of the idea of such a figure, recorded as he is from so many localities.

The cold, dark period of the year had its beginning in Celtic times with the festival of Samhain, the modern Hallowe'en. It was a time when the barriers between this world and the otherworld were let down and communication with the spirits was made possible. It was then that the hunter, in the guise of Woden, Gabriel or Herne, began his wanderings abroad to gather together a spirit throng and guide them to their infernal abode. The "dead" time of the year was a time of fear and superstition and it is not surprising that such beliefs as we have come across in this chapter should all take place during winter.

Thus Herne's role as the Wild Huntsman and his affinity with Woden can be viewed against a wider background of folk belief, a figure recognised and feared across all northern Europe. But as we have seen, this role is only one side of a more complex and composite character and further facets of his nature are yet to be revealed.

The Mask of the Beast

We have seen how humankind in various cultures and stages of development has expressed an affinity with the rest of the natural world, in particular with the animal kingdom. As totemism, ritual hunts and magico-religious rites involving identification with animals and their spirits gradually died out in many parts of the world, especially in the industrialised West, the memory of something lost did not. It is this recollection of the intimate connection between humans and the web of life which has resulted in figures such as the horned god, Herne the Hunter and perhaps the most striking representation of the man-beast which is still very much in evidence today - the hobby horse and its related family of men dressed as animals found in folk customs throughout the world.

Again we return to the prehistoric period, however, to find the earliest example of dressing in animal skins, in fact back to those cave artists of the palaeolithic age. It was in 1869 that the paintings in Altamira in Spain were discovered and for many years they were considered forgeries, but more and more were found, including the famous paintings at Lascaux in France. Consisting of depictions of animals and humans, these paintings are to be found deep inside the caves where they could not possibly have been seen except with the aid of a torch. This, coupled with the fact that many of the human representations appear to be of a ritual nature, makes it seem certain that the paintings were examples of magical or religious expression. The artists were from a hunting culture and we again come across the possibility that these pictures, which mirrored the natural world and its stock of game, were painted as a form of hunting magic to ensure good luck in the chase. This is not likely to be the whole answer, however, and there are probably several reasons for these wonderful paintings to be depicted upon cave walls including, perhaps, sheer artistic enjoyment.

Human figures are not uncommon in these caves and they often appear in what could be interpreted as ritual scenes, and some are clearly in disguise. Such dressing-up takes the form of a man attired in animal

The Sorceror, Cave of Les Trois Frères, after Abbé Breuil

skins of various kinds and wearing an animal headdress. Examples include one figure which bears the head of a mammoth and another that of a bison, complete with horns as well as a tail, who seems to be playing some kind of flute. But the one which is of interest to us in our search for Herne the Hunter is to be found in the Caverne des Trois Frères at Ariège in the French Pyrenees.

Deep into the rock, where it is necessary to walk for half an hour through many passages connecting chambers before reaching our destination, we reach what can only be described as a kind of sanctuary. On our way we have passed many impressive paintings of animals and other figures, but here we find Herne's earliest recorded predecessor. Popularly known as "The Sorceror", he is a human figure about 2 feet high, placed about twelve feet up on the cave wall. But he is a human figure with a difference. Painted in profile, his head is turned towards the observer to reveal round owllike eyes, a long beard, stag's ears and, which is of most interest to us, his head is crowned with a set of antlers. In addition he appears to have the paws of a bear and the tail of a horse, beneath which are prominent male sexual organs. It is only these and his legs which are obviously human and this humanity is also emphasised by the dancing posture in which the artist has placed this strange figure.

Initially he was taken to be a sort of palaeolithic witchdoctor in his ritual costume, but later interpretation saw him as a god who oversaw the hunt and replenishment of game animals. His animal attributes clearly aim to endow him with the characteristics of the creatures concerned and he may well represent the Lord of the Animals. This is reinforced by the many creatures which surround the Sorceror, which include reindeer, horses, asses, mammoths, rhinos, muskox, bears, bison, owls, wolverines and fish. Perhaps the animal features of the Sorceror are, to quote Nikolai Tolstoy, "the psychopomps helping the dancer to be at one again with natural creation before man discovered consciousness and death". That dancing took place within such caves has been suggested by the discovery of an arrangement of footprints in a cave at Le Tuc, indicating a ritual march or dance. Five phallic "sausages" were discovered in a corner of the cave and it may be that these were connected with initiation ceremonies for boys at the age of puberty.

Again, the sexual element and the plentiful depictions of game animals combine to provide a scenario of life, regeneration and plenty, so important to early peoples as well as "primitive" people today. It was to the otherworld or spiritworld of nature that the shaman would make a visit in his ecstatic trance, and perhaps the Sorceror can be seen as the first shaman in history, enacting his ritual in a torchlit cave. Thus we see this antlered figure, this Herne prototype, looking out at us in a dimly lit cavern and we can envisage him as one example of the

The Mask of the Beast

Hypothetical reconstruction of cave rituals in the cave of the Sorceror (from "Beyond the Bounds of History" by Abbé Breuil, 1949)

personification of the power of nature coming down to us over the centuries, revealing itself in modified forms such as the antlered men of Star Carr and Cernunnos, and giving us the local tradition of Herne the Hunter on his Wild Hunt, a hunt which began back in the prehistoric mists of time.

And perhaps we can today see a living echo of those far-off days, for in a Staffordshire village there is still enacted a ritual dance incorporating not only traditional figures and costumes but also antlers. In early September for one day the village of Abbots Bromley sees a remarkable folk custom taking place in its streets. Called the Horn Dance it consists of six dancers who each hold a set of antlers and engage in a folk dance accompanied by a group of other characters. There are three sets of antlers painted white and three painted black attached to skulls fixed to poles about fifteen inches long. These are held by the dancers as they perform their dance, which consists of the two sets of three facing one other and dancing towards each other and back again several times, almost locking horns in the process. After this they form into single file and then into a circle and at the climax they are chased by the other members of the team, one of whom, Robin Hood, pretends to shoot them with arrows.

The antlers, which are over a thousand years old, are reindeer and it is a mystery how they came to be at Abbots Bromley. They are kept during the year at St. Nicholas' church in the village, which is very appropriate since reindeer are popularly associated with the saint. Santa Claus, and his predecessor St. Nicholas, and his relevance to Herne have been discussed in an earlier chapter. St. Nicholas, of course, was Old Nick himself, the Devil or horned one and the keeping of the antlers in a church dedicated to the saint is probably more than fortuitous. It appears that the dance used to take place during the Christmas period, which links it with the Wild Hunt and the time of death and decay awaiting the spring renewal. The dance itself, with its three black and three white antlers, can be seen as the annual fight between the dying god of the old year and the regenerative god of the new, that eternal battle which is fought each year as summer follows winter only to be followed by winter again.

As already shown, the antler became a symbol of fertility and regrowth and its use in the Abbots Bromley Horn Dance around the winter solstice can be no mere coincidence but must represent the spirit of life lying dormant ready to come alive again in the spring. It is interesting to note that, apart from a fool, hobby horse and Maid Marian, one of the other key figures accompanying the dancers is Robin Hood (see footnote). Robert Graves felt that Robin Hood represented the relic of a prehistoric figure once worshipped as a stag, adding that stag's horn moss is sometimes referred to as Robin Hood's hatband. We shall encounter Robin Hood and his role in British myth in the next chapter. The presence of Maid Marian, the she-male or man dressed as a woman common in such customs, is also significant. Whilst the dancing is going on she thrusts a small stick into a ladle in time to the music, an act which has overtly sexual overtones and providing yet another link with sexuality, fertility and antlers.

The custom of dressing up as animals either in the form of hobby horses or wearing some other form of costume such as a mask dates back, as we have seen, to prehistoric times and the tradition of performing these customs during the winter period is well attested. It is perhaps to imitate devilish beings by disguising themselves as semi-bestial that people associated themselves with the underworld, since ghosts and other otherworldly beings were said to roam abroad during winter time, beginning at the Celtic feast of Samhain. This festival in turn became our Hallowe'en with its more frivolous tone.

This sort of activity was frowned upon by the Church and it is through the influence of Christianity that such practices were considered devilish and the work of witchcraft. Indeed it was believed that members of witches' covens often attended their sabbaths dressed in

---

Footnote: Herne made an appearance in H.T.V.'s "Robin of Sherwood" television series of the mid 1980's. The haunting music to this series was recorded as "Legend" by Clannad and features a piece entitled "Herne"

The Mask of the Beast

Abbots Bromley horn dance (Fortean Picture Library)

goats' or stags' skins and wearing horns, and it is probable that the broomstick is allied to the hobby horse. The Devil himself was said to appear on such occasions in the form of an animal, often that of a stag but also as a goat, sheep and other beasts. In the 16c. it is recorded that members of covens claimed to have encountered the Devil in the likeness of a stag and a confession from Conneticut in 1662 stated that the accused saw the Devil in the form of a deer or fawn.

It is apparent from statements confessed at witchtrials that animal masks are being referred to and the body of the participant may well have been dressed in skins. Dressing up in this manner no doubt gave rise to the idea that witches could change their shape and appear as any animal they wished, the hare often being the preferred choice. There is a noteworthy Windsor connection here in that one Father Rosimund was declared to be such a shapeshifter by Elizabeth Stile, one of the Windsor Witches. Father Rosimund, a widower, and his daughter were said to join the Windsor Witches at their meetings and in 1579 Elizabeth Stile confessed that she had seen him sometimes in the form of an ape and sometimes a horse.

Thus this idea of man and animal being linked in some way and the tendency for some kind of expression of this age-old idea has turned up in various forms from the Sorceror of the palaeolithic cave paintings through the witch-god or Devil to the ritual dressing as animals which has survived to this day in many folk customs. An example of this comes from a potsherd found in Colchester. Dating from the Romano-British period, it depicts a woodland scene with men dressed in animal skins and wearing antlers. It appears to be portraying a story or myth of some kind connected with this ancient theme of the man-beast. Herne the Hunter, this fusion of man and stag, features once again this idea and it may well be that there was once a custom long ago in Windsor that included a man dressed as a stag who appeared at the winter solstice to enact the story of the defeat of winter by spring in some form of mummers play or dance.

If such a custom existed, then it would almost certainly have been discouraged or suppressed by the Church. There are many references to the Church acting against these popular activities and it is pertinent to quote a few here, some of which specifically refer to dressing as stags, as does the first example. The 4th century Bishop Pacianus of Barcelona seems to have felt very guilty, as he chided himself for criticising people for disguising themselves as a stag in a folk play. He regretted this decision since he afterwards thought that by describing the disguise he was actively helping people by showing them what to do. What a dilemma for a man of the cloth!

A few years later St. Augustine preached a sermon which encouraged people to severely punish those who took part in the despicable practice of dressing up like a stag or horse. Caesarius of Arles, who lived from 470 to 542 A.D., deplored those who dressed themselves in animal skins or who put on the heads of horned beasts. In the 6th century the Council of Auxerre condemned anyone who, on 1st January, masqueraded as stags or bullcalves.

Moving on to the 7th. century, St. Aldhelm is said to have expressed horror at revellers wearing animal costumes, especially of stags, and around 700 Theodore, Archbishop of Canterbury, reiterated such thoughts. He condemned those who, at the Kalends of January, went about garbed as beasts, clothed in animal skins and putting on the heads of beasts. In particular he complained about those dressed as stags or old women, which he considered devilish and deserved three years' penance. This was echoed on the Continent, where the Vita Sancti Eligii proclaimed that nobody should, again on the Kalends of January, dress as abominable and ridiculous things such as stags, old women or play games. Again these traditions were specific to January, which links them to the winter activities of the Wild Hunt and Herne himself.

The prohibitions continued and in 915 Regino of Prun told his diocese that they had done on January 1st what the pagans do, i.e. gone about as a stag or calf, and he urged them to repent. This was also decreed by Burchard of Worms in 1024, who ordered those who put on stag or calf disguises to do penance for thirty days on bread and water. These proclamations obviously did not stop such revelry as the 14th century manuscript "Le roman d'Alexandre" contains several illustrations depicting people in animal masks including the stag, goat and bull.

We can see from the aforementioned decrees that dressing up and dancing in the disguise of some animal such as a stag was not uncommon in Europe during the Middle Ages. Specific instances can be cited, as an example from Rumania which concerns the equivalent of our mummers shows. In one of their Christmas plays a fool, carrying a phallus, kills a stag. In Iceland we come across the hart dance, which involved a stag with candles on its antlers, who pushed the women into the middle of the room at which part they would sing songs concerning deer. There was also a hind dance, a game whereby a "hind mother" would divide the players into hinds and harts, the latter being blindfolded. It was then up to the harts to choose a hind, whereupon the hind mother would "marry" them. This game is probably a debased modern form of an earlier custom. In Salzburg there was a dance, which appears to be not unlike that of Abbots Bromley, where six dancers carried high frames which simulated antlers and had bells attached.

Further south in the Austrian Tyrol it was the custom at wedding masquerades to don masks and costumes which gave the appearance that satyrs or ghosts were present at the festivities. Chief among these was the Schimmelreiter or the rider on the white horse, who is in reality the Wild Huntsman himself, and it appears that these "guests" represented the Wild Hunt itself. It was probably highly significant that they attended a function which was seen as a prelude to new life and their presence at such an event encouraged fertility in the newlyweds by summoning otherworldly beings and powers.

We have earlier encountered the idea of the wild man and it is appropriate here to examine his role in the folk customs of central Europe, where he often appeared as a character in seasonal plays which featured a hunt. The plays would commence with the rousing of the wild man who would enter in a demented manner, frightening the villagers as he passed by. A hunt soon ensued which culminated in his being taken away bound in chains, thrown in the village pond, borne away on a bier or even being killed. Such theatrical events took place at Twelfth Night or at Carnival (February) and thus can be linked with the Wild Hunt and with other activities which took place at this time of year, as we shall see a little later. The wild man was often accompanied by other members of the Wild Hunt, such as devils, demons and man-beasts. Even as late as 1695 there is a report from Saxony of a pageant including a wild man who appeared between someone wearing a stag mask and another impersonating a kind of demented devil.

Carnival was held intermittently at Nuremberg between 1449 and 1539 and this too featured elements of the Wild Hunt, a contemporary commenting that the mummers' unruly behaviour was "quite demonlike". The Nuremberg wild men were dressed in hairy garb and sported beards, whilst the huntsman was accompanied by demons and masked characters in the form of pigs, storks and goats. The mummers carried evergreen branches, some of which contained a sort of firework gun which added to the wild nature of the custom, the wild man dwelling amongst wild nature, symbolising his role as lightning demon. So rowdy were the antics of the Nuremberg mummers, that a 15c. police order complained about the mummers terrorising the villagers by chasing and beating them and causing damage and other kinds of nuisance.

It has been suggested that being selected to play the role of the wild man at these festivities was rewarded by being accepted into an esoteric group, many of which existed in the Middle Ages. These secret societies would consider themselves as the Wild Hunt itself and would rampage through villages at the appropriate time of the year, especially at Twelfth Night and Carnival and it is of interest to note that Carnival still contained traits of the Wild Hunt after it had become a popular entertainment. However the origins of the wild man and the Wild Hunt in their guise as folk customs are interpreted, there is no doubt as to the ideas lurking beneath the surface. Fertility and rebirth after death are interwoven into the drama and the demise of the winter demon in order to free the regrowth of nature in the spring are at the core of the festivities. Thus we see once again Herne speaking to us, as the similarities between him, the wild man, the Wild Hunt and Carnival do not need to be emphasised as they are all clear aspects of the same theme.

Returning to animal disguises, the most common both in Europe and Britain is that of the horse and we have seen that a hobby horse accompanied the Abbots Bromley dancers. There are two main types of horse disguise, one being the "man-horse" where the "rider" wears around his waist a light framework over which is draped a coloured cloth which hangs almost to the ground. At either end is attached a horse's head and a tail. Perhaps one of the best known is that at Minehead, Somerset, which is brightly coloured and appears on May Day. Also on this day appears the Padstow 'Obby 'Oss, a very individual hobby horse which dances through the town accompanied by a Teaser who dances in front and encourages the 'Oss to copy. The whole event is accompanied also by much music, singing and other activities.

The other kind of horse disguise is described in Kent as the Hooden Horse. This type is often made from a horse's skull and would be fixed to a pole held by a man covered by some form of blanket. The lower jaw was hinged, enabling the Hoodener to make it snap. Accompanied by other characters, the Hooden Horse would emerge at midwinter and make the round of the village streets with much singing, normally carols, and would chase and snap at young women. A related example comes from South Wales and was known as the Mari Llwyd, which consisted of a horse's skull with its operator covered by a white sheet. The idea here was to gain entrance to a house by singing traditional rhymes, those inside the house trying to outdo those in the Mari Llwyd's group, which consisted of another collection of strange characters. Once inside, the Mari Llwyd would prance about neighing and teasing the women. Again this custom would take place around Christmas.

There is much discussion as to the origin of the word "Hooden", some saying that it derives from "wooden" and others from "hooded", referring to the fact that the operator of the snapping jaw is actually hooded. There is another alternative, however, which may provide a link with Herne. The origin may come from "Woden", i.e. giving us

Woden's Horse and it must be remembered that Woden was himself a hooded figure. The Horse would then be imbued with the spirit of the god whose name, as we saw earlier, derived from a root meaning mad or furious. The horse's actions at these customs were often of a wild nature and much of the custom would consist of the fact that the horse was unwelcome, and this applied both to the Hooden Horse and other varieties.

The Salisbury Hob-Nob, which used to appear in the streets on great occasions in the company of a giant, would snap at people's clothes and tear them and then chase the unfortunate victims into a canal. The Old Ball of Blackburn used to snap people's fingers in its jaw and had a reputation for sending women into hysterics, and the tail of the Minehead horse would trap those who did not give money. One Hooden Horse in Kent is even reputed to have frightened a woman to death in 1840. When activated, the horse appears to acquire a character of its own, even to its operator, and its unruly antics may well be connected with the wild attributes of Woden, leader of the Wild Hunt and thus with Herne the Hunter. Just as Herne "shakes a chain in a most hideous and dreadful manner", so do the hooderners cavort and carry on, making much noise with such objects as chains, horns and whistles.

Another strange mask was that of the Dorset Ooser which was in the form of a frightening face with large eyes and bearing ox horns. Its context is unclear, but it appears that several were in use in Dorset, but by the early 20c. the last one had been lost. By the 19c. it had become the Christmas Bull which wandered the streets of Dorset villages scaring the inhabitants and demanding refreshments from them. Note again the time of year, the winter solstice period when many of these half men - half animals appeared. When the Lady Godiva festival at Southam took place it is not known, but in the 18c its procession was led by a man wearing the mask of a bull complete with horns, who was known as Old Brazen Face. This could well represent the power of the sun, with the bull symbolising the sun god and Godiva a fertility goddess.

Using antlers as a symbolic display also has its place in British tradition

The Mask of the Beast

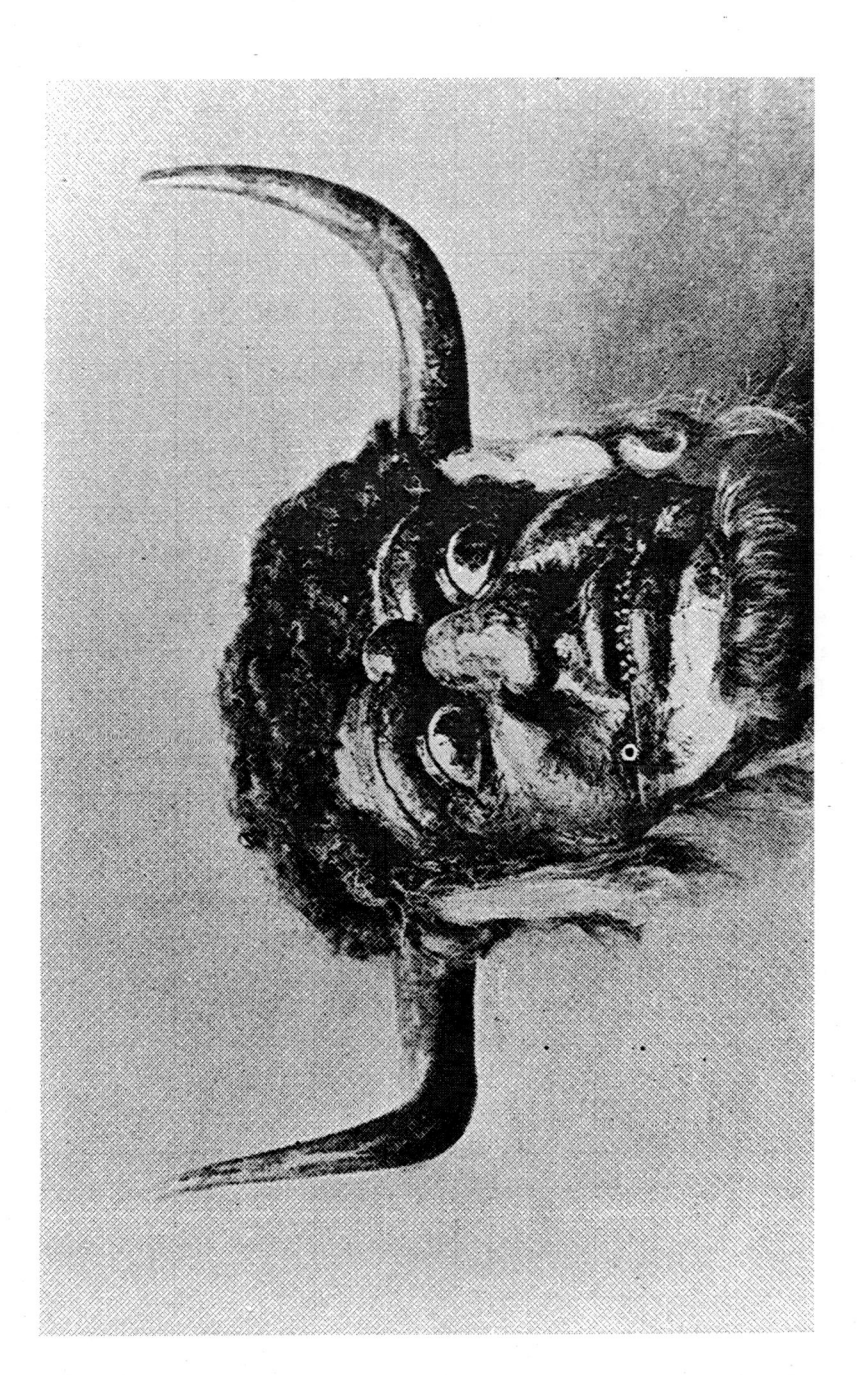

The Dorset Ooser (Fortean Picture Library)

The Mask of the Beast

and although not used strictly as a mask, they were utilised in the custom of Riding the Stang. In cases where a man had been cuckolded, the husband and wife were seated back to back upon a donkey, accompanied by the blowing of trumpets, the beating of drums and other noises in a procession which included stags' antlers and cow horns stuck on the tops of poles. Attached to these would be sheets or items of clothing which would flap about in the air. This custom was practised in the north of England, but there is another which took place in the West Country which again involved the stag, indeed it was called the Stag Hunt.

This used to take place on the wedding night of a couple about whom there had been some scandal. The tradition entailed a man impersonating a stag by placing antlers on his head just like Herne and hanging a bloodfilled bladder beneath his chin. The other members of the group consisted of a huntsman, complete with scarlet coat and hunting horn, and a band of yelping boys. The "hunt" proceeded with much noise through the streets until the couple's house was reached, whereupon the huntsman blew a blast on his horn over the fallen stag and then slit the bladder allowing the blood to spill over the threshold. As can be seen from these two examples they are centred on sexual misdemeanour and we have already come across the connection of antlers with sexuality. The second example is of special interest to us, however, in that here we have an antler-bedecked man involved in a kind of Wild Hunt, although this figure is the hunted not, as in the case of Herne, the hunter.

So it is clear from the examples in this chapter that there is a strong, and ancient, tradition in Britain, and elsewhere, of the man-beast, be it a primitive shaman figure painted on a cave wall or a modern mummer. Thus the idea of a man becoming one with an animal has been in the mind of men for a very long time, ancient man believing that the one could change into the other and vice-versa. The Celts were great believers in shape-shifting, where a human changed into animal form. In Welsh mythology, Gwydion was turned successively into a stag, sow and wolf by Math his uncle. It was in animal form that Gwydion actually fathered offspring. Animals themselves were thought to be imbued with supernatural powers and the fixing of antlers upon Herne's head no doubt symbolised the passing on of this power to him in order to regain his strength. The power contained within a set of antlers was no doubt behind the action of the Witch of Berkeley. As part of the protection she needed against being carried off by the Devil, it was necessary for her to be wrapped in a stag's skin, although even this proved ineffectual against the might of Satan. The story represents, nevertheless, the continuity of the belief in the efficacy and symbolism of dressing in animal masks and costumes.

The appearance of many animal masks at Christmas and during the winter period ties them to Herne's appearances which also are traditionally said to occur at this time, as is the Wild Hunt. They can be viewed as being aspects of the same idea of the regenerative aspect of nature fighting its way through the bleak winter period, driving away the darkness and taking with it the souls of the departed to leave the land ready to begin anew in the spring. Perhaps Herne and his antlers are a folk memory of a custom involving animal masks, much in the vein of Padstow's 'Obby 'Oss, the Abbots Bromley Horn Dance or possibly a mummer's play. These plays often include the idea of a death and resurrection representing the waning of the old year and the waxing of the new. Herne's story certainly fits in with this concept, which is explored in the following chapter.

Death and Sacrifice

The voluntary death of Herne upon the old oak has so much in common with pagan myth, and in particular with the fate of Woden, that it is worth investigating the parallel further. The two chief, constant points in the variations on the Herne story are that: (a) he appears wearing antlers and (b) he hanged himself from an oak tree. This second point is of great significance in the quest for Herne's origins.

> I am aware that I hung
> On the windswept tree,
> for nine days and nights;
> I was pierced by a spear
> and given to Woden,
> myself made offering to myself.

These are the opening lines concerning Woden's self-sacrifice from Havamal, one of the Verse Edda or ancient Icelandic poems which are steeped in Northern mythology. Havamal means "the words of the High One", i.e. Woden, and is a collection of verses in the form of charms and proverbs. The section which concerns us here tells how Woden hung from the World Ash, Yggdrasil, for nine days, how he was wounded by a spear, how he was given no food or drink and how he grasped the runes and acquired a hidden knowledge.

Runes were the magical alphabet used by the Germanic tribes of Northern Europe and each character consisted of various combinations of straight lines, which reveals that they were originally carved into wood upon which it was more difficult to effect round symbols. In fact Tacitus confirms this, as well as telling us that they were originally used for divinatory purposes. He describes the casting of lots whereby the branch of a tree is cut off and slit into strips which are then inscribed with individual runes. These are then cast randomly and, after a prayer to the gods, three are picked up and the meanings of the selected runes read. Although used for magical purposes, they were later used for inscriptions and there are a few Viking examples to be found in Britain.

One of the finest collections to be found anywhere are inside the neolithic tomb of Maes Howe on Mainland Orkney, inscribed when Vikings entered the tomb three thousand years after its construction. The Anglo-Saxons also used their own version of the runic alphabet, but recorded instances are not common.

After he had so acquired the wisdom, Woden then cut magical runes upon his spear, upon Sleipnir's teeth and upon a bear's claws. This is interesting, for during excavations at Viking Dublin during the 1970's a number of objects were discovered containing runic inscriptions including a piece of antler. The runes read "hurn:hiartar", meaning "hart's horn" which is apt but does not tell us anything more than what is obvious (note also the Viking spelling of horn "hurn"). Woden is also associated with runes, or glory-twigs as they were also known, in an Anglo-Saxon verse entitled the "Nine Herbs Charm". In this Woden is said to have thrown nine glory-twigs at a crawling adder, scattering it into nine parts. Perhaps here we have another connection with Herne and his chain, as we now see both Cernunnos and Woden having serpentine assocations.

Woden's spell hanging on the tree led him to be known as Hangatyr or God of the Hanged as well as Galgatyr or Gallows God. It was the custom to make sacrifices to Woden and stabbed victims were hung from trees in the god's honour throughout the Germanic world, especially at the temple at Uppsala in Sweden, where the practice continued until the 10c. Enemy captives were hanged in honour of Woden and, in time of need it may have been considered apposite to sacrifice a king who was dedicated to the god. In fact there are indications that the Swedish kings held office for periods of nine years, at the end of which period they were killed. However substitutes were sometimes found and King Aun is said to have asked of Woden how long he would reign and was given the answer that it would be as long as he sacrificed a son every ninth year. He apparently carried this out in the case of nine sons, but was prevented by his subjects from killing his last. His time therefore came and he was laid to rest under a mound at Uppsala.

Death and Sacrifice

The description of Woden's sufferings represent the initiation of a shaman into the secrets of esoteric wisdom, the initiate having to undergo a ritual death and rebirth in order to acquire the knowledge he needs to carry out his work. The World Tree was a central feature of shamanistic thought. It connected earth with both heaven and the otherworld and during the shaman's ecstatic trance he would climb his symbolic World Tree which would have consisted of some kind of pole. Thus Woden's experience on Yggdrasil was as willing sacrifice in order to gain the knowledge he required and can be seen in a similar light to the action of Herne as he hung himself on the oak tree. He had lost his woodcraft skills and also his job as a result. His solution was to sacrifice himself to thereby regain his woodland knowledge and thereafter he had successful hunting during those nocturnal rides through Windsor Forest.

The idea of human sacrifice is well attested in many cultures and in prehistoric times the practice of killing the king, dismembering his body and burying the pieces in the ground in order to promote the fertility of the land and the tribe was widespread. The myth of the Egyptian god Osiris is an example of this. When the Egyptians sowed their crops they mourned the death of Osiris, whom they considered they were burying, the seeds being fragments of his body. This is also the case with the Greek god Dionysus who was torn to pieces at Thebes, and the similar deaths of kings Pentheus and Lycurgus in the Greek myths are probably distorted memories of sacrificial kings who died in honour of the god. Another instance is the myth of Actaeon, described earlier, wherein he was killed by his pack of hounds. Adonis, Attis or Tammuz was another god whose death and resurrection represented the annual round of decay and renewal. Worshipped in ancient Greece and Western Asia, his death was mourned each year accompanied by much wailing and music. Images of the god as a corpse dressed in a red robe were annointed with oil and then cast into the sea or a spring. He was mourned with hope, however, since his rebirth was looked forward to. Adonis was Aphrodite's lover and, after being killed by a boar whilst hunting, the goddess secured his release from the underworld for six months of the year. The symbolism of the death of winter alternating with the life of summer is clear.

Death and Sacrifice

Of course the most well known of such sacrifices in our own culture is that of Christ who, like Woden, hung from a tree, or more specifically a wooden cross. There has been speculation that the poem telling of Woden's sufferings was influenced by Christian teachings, but it is now generally agreed that Woden's fate emanates from an independent European tradition with its own primitive roots. Indeed it can be pointed out that one of the reasons why the Jews rejected Christianity was, apart from being blasphemous in that it was claimed that Christ was divine, it also used a blatantly pagan concept of a god being killed for the good of his people and then being resurrected. The fact that this also happened at Easter, when the pagan ceremonies of the spring rebirth and regeneration took place, only acted to confirm in the Jewish mind the paganism of this new faith.

There is another local tradition which has some bearing on the death/rebirth theme and that is the Chalvey Stab-Monk. This consists of the plaster cast of an organ-grinder's monkey said to have been killed by an irate father after it had bitten his child. Up until the First World War it was the custom to parade this effigy around Chalvey, now a part of Slough, accompanied by blackfaced mourners and to stage a mock funeral, burial and wake. Michael Bayley feels that this tradition, with its strong element of death and rebirth, is so reminiscent of the god's death and interment that it must be a relic of a prehistoric sacrificial rite. Thus the idea of death and renewal has never been far from the Windsor locality, Chalvey being just across the Thames, and so Herne's own demise can now be seen in the context of local beliefs which predate the coming of Christianity.

The death of the sacred king is a theme which is relevant to a historical enigma which has parallels with Herne's story. It concerns William the Conqueror's son William II, or William Rufus, who reigned from 1087 to 1100 and who died in what could be described as strange circumstances. The events surrounding the king's death have been interpreted by Dr. Margaret Murray in a manner which surprised the academic world and caused conventional historians to dismiss the theory almost out of hand.

Death and Sacrifice

Dr. Murray, who died at the age of 100 in 1963, was an Egyptologist by training but she also delved into esoteric subjects especially witchcraft, about which she wrote two well known books "The God of the Witches" and "The Witch Cult in Western Europe". Connected to these two books was another entitled "The Divine King in England", which set out to prove that pagan practices, including human sacrifice, lingered on well into Christian times and that some of the victims were well known historical figures. She claimed that witchcraft, which survived into the 17c., was really the "Old Religion" or pagan predecessor of Christianity which was driven underground by the new faith and treated as devilish and evil. Although she may have overstated her case somewhat, since her writings, many neo-pagan groups have sprung up throughout the country who practise the ancient craft of Wicca, as the Saxons called it. Such groups for the most part practise what may be termed white magic and have no connection with anti-Christian devil worshippers or black magicians, although the two often become confused in the media.

Returning to William Rufus, Dr. Murray's thesis claimed that he worshipped the old pagan gods, which was reflected in his noncommittal attitude to the Church, (the Church refused to grant his body the last rites) and that he expected to die for his people. He met his death on 2nd August whilst out stag hunting, killed by the arrow fired by a knight named Walter Tirel. There are several points which are deemed to be significant in this story. The first is the date, which happens to be the day after Lammas, which was a Christianisation of the pagan Celtic festival of Lughnasad, celebrated in honour of the god Lugh. August 1st was the day when the death of Lugh was commemorated, who was seen to be the corn-king who died when the crops were harvested. Lammas was a festival kept as a time of mourning and thus it appears to be appropriate that William's death occurred at this particular moment. Ritual murder or not, there were quite extraordinary scenes of popular demonstrations when William's body was borne on a harvest cart twenty miles to his place of burial at Winchester. Apparently the king's blood "watered the earth all of the way", an expression that could step right out of a pagan bible, should there be such a thing.

Secondly, he died at the age of 42, which is a multiple of the mystic number seven. This special number also occurs with respect to an event which is seen as important to the theory. Seven years into his reign, i.e. in 1094, the Archbishop of Canterbury fled to France, apparently because he was chosen to die as a substitute for the King. Then in 1100 William's illegitimate nephew was killed on May 1st, another ancient pagan feast day, and the theory goes on to say that this was inadequate and the king himself had to die at the next opportunity, which happened to be at Lammas. And lastly, as William knew that his end was near, he made preparations for his successor, which is seen by the ease and speed with which Henry I was made king. In addition, William's death was known both throughout England and on the Continent on that very day and portents had already foretold the event which then became widely expected.

The way in which William met his death has connections with Herne's story since William also embarked upon a stag hunt. It was during the hunt that an arrow of his wounded a stag, which then ran off only to be pursued by Tirel, who also took a shot at it. However, his arrow bounced off the animal's antlers, or some say an oak tree, and hit the king who quickly broke off the end and then fell on the shaft. (An oak called the Rufus Oak used to grow near the spot of William's death, the site now being occupied by a memorial known as Rufus's Stone). Another version has it that the king's bowstring broke and he called out to Tirel to let loose one of his own arrows, whereupon the knight did as he was told with the same result.

This story, like Herne's, involves a willing sacrifice and there may well be an element of truth in it, although historians would place more conventional interpretations on William's death. The king's nickname "Rufus", however, is an enigma. It is Latin for red and may have referred to the colour of his hair. Red is also symbolic of fertility and vigour and Rufus may therefore symbolise the old religion through its god-king. Although there is much that is contentious in this story it is in the same vein as that of Herne the Hunter, incorporating the idea of a sacrificial death and involving those potent symbols of the stag and oak. Another king, Edmund the Martyr, was also said to have met his death

Death and Sacrifice

in the vicinity of an oak tree. In 870 he was apparently tied to this oak at Hoxne in Suffolk and shot with arrows by the Danes, and the tree survived to the mid 19c.

In the case of Herne there is a variation on the theme, for in his tale Herne can be seen to act as a substitute for the king, dying in his place to achieve the aim of ensuring the continued good fortune of his land and people. And surely this is what lies behind the legend of Herne the Hunter, even though later elements such as the Wild Hunt, have been grafted on to the story. The religious ideas behind this are worth investigating and we can do no better than examining their place in ancient Greece as postulated by Robert Graves.

The ancient Greeks were a mixture of the patriarchal Hellenes, who invaded Greece in the second millennium B.C., and the goddess-worshipping native Pelasgians. Although the Hellenes had attempted to impose their culture upon the Pelasgians, a compromise was reached whereby they accepted the idea of matrilinear succession and became the children of the Great Goddess, to whom they provided sacred kings. The king was chosen to represent a god such as Zeus or Poseidon and Graves has shown that many of the Greek myths tell of the merging of the god worshippers and goddess worshippers or the taking over of the latter by the former.

The evolution of kingship and its role within the religious system of the Greeks shows how the king progressed from sacrificial victim to ruler of the tribe. At the beginning the tribal Nymph, or representative of the goddess, would take a lover each year to become her king, who then became a fertility symbol and who was sacrificed when his reign finished at the year end. After the ritual killing, the king's blood would have been sprinkled over crops, trees and animals to ensure fertility in the coming year. His soul was then free to enter the strong body of his successor, for to wait until he died a natural death would have left the king's soul weak and exhausted and an easy prey for demons.

The next stage of development concerned the king's association with the sun, which was seen to decline after midsummer, and it was at this time of his death that another king, the tanist or twin, took over to be sacrificed in turn at midwinter. Later the limiting of his reign to one year proved unsatisfactory to the incumbent and the reign was extended. However, the fertility of the land still had to be ensured and another compromise was agreed upon. Now the king underwent a mock death and for one day only yielded his kingship to a surrogate who at the end of the day suffered the ritual death.

The exact nature of the sacrifice varied according to local tradition and circumstances. Examples include drowning, burning, being struck in the heel by a poisoned arrow, being axed, being ripped to pieces by intoxicated women and being thrown over a cliff. Whatever the method it was imperative that the king must die, a practice which it is said continued up until Celtic times. Indeed Julius Caesar reports that the Druids practised human sacrifice and burned prisoners of war in huge wicker baskets in the shape of a human figure, but how much this is exaggeration is difficult to say. The Roman writers such as Caesar were writing from a biased point of view, but there is no doubt that they saw the Druids as a force to be reckoned with and they ruthlessly stamped out Druidism in Britain at Anglesey where, in 60 A.D., the last remaining remnants of the order were put to death by the Romans amid much cursing. How much this was instigated by the abhorrence of human sacrifice is debatable but there was more than a touch of fear that the Druids represented a pan-tribal force which could stir up Celtic nationalism amongst the separate tribes.

Which brings us to a British sacrifice, or so it is seen, which has been much in the archaeological news in recent years - Lindow Man. Discovered in a Cheshire peat bog in 1984, Lindow Man, or Peat Marsh as he is popularly known, was found by peat diggers, although only the top half of the body was retrieved intact. Luckily this was from the abdomen, which meant that the contents of his stomach could be analysed. He is presumed to date from the late iron age, like many bodies found in similar circumstances in Danish bogs, the most famous being Tollund Man who had been strangled and thrown into the bog in about 210 B.C. In the case of Lindow Man, he had been struck hard on the back of the head, garotted and then his throat had been cut before

Death and Sacrifice

being left for dead in a pool of water. Although there is some confusion of radio carbon dates, there is general consensus that he dates from the first century A.D.

What was so interesting about Lindow Man's body was its condition at the time of death. He was a well-built man aged 25-30 who had obviously been well fed. His nails had been well cared for and it was apparent that he did not come from the lower orders of society but from some higher caste, perhaps from the aristocracy or even from the Druids themselves. Dr. Anne Ross and Dr. Don Robins have suggested that he was a Druidic prince who had been put to death in 60 A.D. as a sacrifice to the gods in the wake of the Roman onslaught. Mistletoe, that plant so highly regarded by the Druids, was found in pollen form in his stomach adding to the idea that here we are looking at the result of a ritual murder. It could well be that he was sacrificed to three Celtic gods who demanded sacrifices - Taranis by beheading or stunning, Esus by slit throats and Teuttades by drowning. There were no signs of other physical violence or of a struggle and it therefore appears that here we have a well bred, chosen and willing victim offered as a sacrifice for his people. The parallels with Herne are not so obvious here, although the ritual death is prominent in both but Herne's privileged position after his cure could well be seen as being similar to the obviously groomed Lindow Man, the quasi-royal substitute who gave his life in the place of the king.

Another parallel with Herne and sacred victims concerns the myth of Orion the Hunter, son of the Greek god Poseidon. Orion met up with the goddess Artemis, the Huntress, and they spent many hours together enjoying the chase. However, Artemis' brother, Apollo, learnt of this liaison and was concerned that their partnership could lead to a serious relationship. He therefore tricked Artemis into unwittingly shooting Orion with an arrow whereupon, discovering what she had done, she implored Apollo's son, Asclepius, to restore him to life. However, before he was able to revive the great hunter, he was struck by a thunderbolt sent by Zeus. This myth again reiterates the theme of the sacred king who, acting for a period as consort of the goddess, is then ritually slain.

It also appears that Artemis herself was a sacrificial victim for, in her sacred grove in Arcadia, an effigy of the goddess was hanged each year and she was thus known as the Hanged One. Similar rites involving a hanged female are recorded at Ephesus in Asis Minor and Melite in Greece. At Melite virgins annually hanged a young goat in front of Artemis' image, probably acting as a substitute for a human sacrifice. Helen of Troy was worshipped on the island of Rhodes as Helen of the Tree, since she was said to have been hung on a tree by the Queen of Rhodes' handmaidens.

The Orion myth is of special interest also in that it incorporates two other key elements from the Herne story. The first concerns Asclepius, the god of healing, who not only healed the sick and became the founder of the medicinal arts but was also said to be able to raise the dead. He is thus very similar to Urswick in Herne's story, though the latter succeeded in his healing of Herne whilst in the case of Orion, Asclepius failed, although his powers were not weakened when he brought King Lycurgus back to life. Lycurgus had killed his own son Dryas by cutting him down with an axe whilst under the impression he was cutting a vine. Dryas means "oak" and thus here is another example of the substitute being sacrificed in the place of the king, Dryas being the oak king who was slain annually. In this case, however, Lycurgus' land grew barren and he in turn was put to death and was pulled apart by wild horses. Asclepius' involvement in this story is all the more relevant since his name means "that which hangs from the oak" and refers to mistletoe, whose berries' white viscous juice was considered by the Druids to be oak-sperm and important as a symbol of regeneration. Such concepts may well underlie Herne's death upon an oak tree and it is significant that Asclepius was struck by a thunderbolt just as Herne's Oak was blasted by lightning.

Urswick is an intriguing figure in the Herne story and can be likened, perhaps, to characters such as Gandalf in Tolkien's Lord of the Rings and to that Arthurian magician Merlin. He is as mysterious as these characters, living alone as he does in his forest hut and appearing out of nowhere at time of need. Indeed, he can be viewed as a shaman or even a Druid, both of which were healers amongst other things. It may be that he is in fact a folk memory of some pagan priest who officiated in the distant past at rites which involved worship of the horned god. As an oak cult survived well into Saxon times and the idea of a horned figure was still worshipped during the Roman period, it is not impossible that in the character of Urswick we are seeing the shadows of pre-Christian Druidical priests who led a local cult in Windsor Forest. The placing of antlers on Herne's head may represent a rite wherein the chief priest donned a set of antlers in his guise as the object of worship, the horned god he who heals and lords it over the natural world in his role as master of life and death.

Returning to classical mythology, the myth of Hercules and the Ceryneian hind is relevant here. As one of the famous Twelve Labours of Hercules, his third was to capture the Ceryneian hind and to bring her back alive. This animal had brazen hooves and golden antlers and she was sacred to Artemis. It took the hero one year in which to capture this wondrous beast. Robert Graves refers to this story as telling of the capture of a shrine where Artemis was worshipped in her guise of Elaphios, meaning "hindlike". He considered that the four stags which pulled her chariot represented the four years of an Olympiad at the end of which a sacrificial victim dressed in deerskins was ritually hunted and killed. One version of the story states that the hind was dedicated to the goddess by one of the Pleiades to thank her for disguising her as a hind to avoid the amorous Zeus. Unfortunately, this did not work and after her seduction she hanged herself. Yet again we come across the recurring themes of deer, oaks, sacrifices, hunting and hanging which are so important in the tale of Herne the Hunter.

The antlered king and his death have been told via the story of Actaeon in an earlier chapter. The tale represents the annual sacrifice of the sacred king and the taking on of a new lover/consort by the goddess's representative. Such an antlered god was Cernunnos and it is via his worship we arrive at the legend of Britain's most famous folk hero after Arthur - Robin Hood. It has already been pointed out in chapter 6 that Robin Hood himself was once worshipped as a stag god and the name Robin was identified with witches as shown in a pamphlet published in 1639 which depicts "Robin Goodfellow" as a god worshipped by a

Death and Sacrifice

coven. He is portrayed as a bearded man with the lower half of his body in the form of a goat. He has horns, is ithyphallic, holds a candle in one hand and a besom in the other and stands in the middle of a circle made up of eleven people holding hands with a twelfth playing a pipe. Robin was the name given to the Devil by medieval witches and Dr. Margaret Murray felt that this lent support to her idea that witchcraft was a survival of the old religion which revered a horned god.

Robin later became confused with a historical figure, that of the 14c. outlaw Robin Hood of Sherwood Forest. He seems to have become associated with May Day revels and his band of merry men formed a coven with Maid Marian as the coven's maid who was Robin's bride in the May orgies which still took place at this time and were not finally abandoned until repressed by the Puritans in the 17c. It has been suggested that Robin's surname is derived from the hood or mask he wore during the May revels and that this may be a survival of the rituals of a cult connected with Woden. It could be that once upon a time the May festivities, seeing as they were largely about summer growth and the promise of a healthy harvest, could have partly originated in ceremonies honouring Woden. As well as being a god of the dead, he was also a god of fertility.

Robin is associated with the forest, and the colour of his costume - green - also reveals him to be a variation on the Green Man who stood for the spirit of nature. As well as Robin Hood, this figure was also known as Robin of the Wood, King of the May and Jack in

Robin Goodfellow, a 17c illustration

Death and Sacrifice

the Green and was a prominent feature of May celebrations. Ian Taylor says "Robin Hood is the Green Man, the power-in-Nature aspect of the male principle of creation. He is the terrestrial aspect of the ancient horned god of the Underworld". The man chosen to take on the part was covered in a wickerwork frame from head to foot and interleaved amongst the frame were greenery, flowers and ribbons with a slit left open for him to see. As with antlers, the Green Man represented the regenerative spirit and new life re-emerging from winter's death. It became such a potent image that, despite its pagan origins, it has left its image in numerous churches throughout the land. A visit to many an ancient church will often reward the visitor with carvings of human faces which either sprout greenery from their mouths or are actually made of foliage. And who knows how many pubs named "The Green Man" are scattered throughout England?

The Green Man has affinities, therefore, with the antlered god, both of them being symbols of regeneration and also representing the wild, untamed side of nature which surrounds humankind and of which we are inextricably a part. Related to this concept is that of the Wild Man, found in many ancient mythologies as well as in medieval art and literature. Perhaps the earliest example is the figure of Enkidu in the Babylonian epic of the third millennium B.C., Gilgamesh. He is described as being covered in hair and feeding and drinking with the wild beasts. Whatever the cultural context, however, the Wild Man is portrayed as being devoid of all civilised feeling, having a crude sexuality and being a hunter who kills and eats his game raw, as do animals. In the middle ages he was known as Wodewose, from the Saxon words meaning "wild man of the woods", and depictions of such a figure can be found carved under misericords, on bench-ends, on fonts and in other places in many of our churches and cathedrals.

One example of this type of character can be found close to home in the form of Merlin, that wizard extraordinaire of Arthurian mythology. Geoffrey of Monmouth in his "History of the Kings of Britain" describes Merlin's madness where he left his fellow men and retired to the woods. He ate fruit, berries and grass and became like a wild animal. It is this semibestial quality which likens the Wild Man to

Death and Sacrifice

Herne the Hunter, the untamed half man half animal that rages through the forest proclaiming savage nature in all her glory.

Merlin bears many resemblances to the horned god, both, for example, having supernatural power over wild animals. Like Cernunnos, Merlin was associated with certain animals, such as the wolf, pig and most importantly the stag. In Geoffrey of Monmouth's "Life of Merlin" there occurs a striking episode when Merlin discovers that his wife, Guendoloena, was about to marry another husband. He immediately gathered together a herd of deer and rode with these to the wedding upon a stag. When he arrived, he promptly tore the antlers from his stag and hurled them at the bridegroom, crushing his head and killing him outright. Merlin then rode back into the forest on the mutilated stag, but fell off whilst trying to cross a river and was captured and taken back.

Now it may seem a strange and perhaps sickening act upon Merlin's part to have torn off the stag's antlers, but Nikoloi Tolstoy in his "Quest for Merlin" suggests an explanation for this otherwise vicious act. He surmises that it is not the stag's antlers that he removes so violently, but a set which, like Herne, he is wearing on his own head and that the transfer to the stag occurred at an earlier stage through a misunderstanding. Thus here we see Merlin, Herne and Cernunnos as aspects of one and the same figure, the Lord of the Animals, the dweller in the forest, the antlered one. The idea of the horned god was very strong in the Celtic world of our ancestors so much so that it has remained a part of our folk tradition in the form of Merlin and Herne. They represent elemental, otherworld beings who lord it over nature, who lead a wild band and who ultimately degenerate into a magician, the Devil or some ghostly spirit as the centuries pass by.

The stag figure is not restricted to Herne and Merlin in British mythology, however, for other examples can be cited. In Irish myth, Tuan Mac Cairill was turned into a stag, a boar, an eagle and a salmon, after having survived a catastrophe which overcame the Irish people. As he slept one night be began to prophesy future events and then felt himself metamorphose into a stag. He became aware of two antlers with three score points grow upon his head and his form became rough and grey. He then became the leader of Ireland's deer herds and a large band of stags followed him wherever he went. Then he became old and again felt another transformation coming on, this time into that of a boar and after becoming an eagle and a salmon he eventually regained his human shape.

In the romance of Owain from the Mabinogion, Owain encounters a Black Man on top of a mound, who has one foot, one eye in the middle of his forehead and wields an iron club. Around him are one thousand wild animals and Owain asks him what power he had over them. As an answer he struck a stag with the club at which it let out a great roar, which caused all the animals to come together so that it was difficult to stand amongst them. The Black Man then ordered them to go and feed, whereupon they bowed before him as to a lord. Again the recurring themes of stags and a wild man who has power over animals.

The Mabinogion furnishes us with a further tale of stags and sacrifices. It was outside the castle of Lleu Llaw Gyffes that one Gronw Bebyr was seen to be pursuing a stag, together with his huntsmen and dogs. Eventually the stag grew tired, the dogs brought it down and Gronw killed it. Robert Graves sees the stag as symbolising Lleu himself and that this is another example of the sacred king being killed and replaced by his successor in the annual round.

The ritual slaying of the king, and later a substitute, for his people, seems to have been the practice in most ancient cultures. Sometimes the substitute was a member of the royal family and the first born was often considered to be suitable. The Biblical story of Abraham and Isaac comes to mind here, no doubt recalling a folk memory of the days when human sacrifices took place rather than those of rams. And later on the New Testament provides us with a further example of the sacrifice of the god-king in the person of Jesus Christ. Whatever the interpretation of Christ's life and death, he was certainly termed by the Romans "King of the Jews" and the idea of the young god overcoming death and being restored to the land of the living to renew nature's life feature strongly in the background of the Gospel story. As E.O. James puts it, "In Christian tradition this theme of the dying and reviving Year-god was brought into relation with that of the conquering Christ under the apocalyptic symbolism of the lamb slain sacrificially from the foundation of the world to ensure that final triumph of good over evil and of life over death".

Thus by returning to Christ on the Cross, we arrive back again at Herne hanging from the oak, dying, perhaps, in the place of his king, if the ancient underlying themes can be once more restored. In a sense, however, Herne died twice, for he was brought back to life by Urswick after being gored by the stag. But, if the story can be read in this way, Herne's powers were not restored but began to wane and there was therefore only one answer - self sacrifice. If there were other elements representing regeneration and fertility in the tale, they were obviously suppressed long ago, but what remains is highly suggestive that the story of Herne the Hunter was that of the age-old theme of the annual cycle of the seasons and their importance to early man. And it is perhaps at his peril that modern man ignores his ties with the natural world and sees it merely as an object to be plundered and polluted.

A Fiendish Phantom

The spectral appearances of Herne the Hunter have much in common with other ghostly manifestations, the chief difference of course, being the wearing of the antlers. As described in Chapter 3, there are wild hunts recorded in many areas of Britain and abroad and ghosts wielding chains are too numerous to mention. A brief note on ghosts, however, is appropriate here to provide a framework for putting Herne into perspective and to try and ascertain what kind of ghost he is.

There are various theories as to the nature of ghosts and perhaps, like those other elusive phenomena, U.F.O.'s, there may be a number of causes, depending on the type of manifestation. Traditionally ghosts have been regarded as spirits of the dead, especially of those who met an unfortunate end involving such dramatic events as murders and suicides. It appears that such spirits, however their actual nature is defined, are earthbound and remain at the spot that the original event occurred. Another explanation is known as the tape-recorder theory, which involves a traumatic event "imprinting" itself on its immediate surroundings, usually but not always a building, and being "played back" under certain circumstances. There is much to commend T.C. Lethbridge's theory of "psyche fields", which involve the thoughtforms of one individual becoming impressed into the static field of, say, a building, tree or other place, and then being picked up at some future date by third parties. Alternatively, manifestation may occur as a result of telepathic communication either by the person who is experiencing an event acting as a transmitter or by someone observing that event. Often, though, ghosts of whatever type are seen only by psychics who are attuned to wavelengths closed to many of us.

Herne is no ordinary ghost, however, and even though he shares certain aspects of the aforementioned, he cannot be rigidly categorised. Joan Forman has analysed supernatural apparitions into ten types and Herne the Hunter falls into that which she describes as a "primitive, archaic or racial memory manifestation". Examples of this type include such figures as Black Shuck from East Anglia and the Wild Hunt itself, led by whoever the local huntsman happens to be. Such ghosts represent a deep, unconscious memory of the past and its history or prehistory and, as such, question whether modern humankind has really cut itself off from its roots. Herne's appearances also overlap somewhat with another of her categorisations, i.e. the "single event" where a dramatic event took place, in this instance Herne's suicide. In the case of Herne, however, we have a ghost whose appearances do not fit exactly into any category, since he is traditionally said to appear during the winter months, but in recent times has heralded times of national crisis, irrespective of the time of year.

Herne's suicide also has much in common with that of another figure associated with Windsor Great Park. At the southern end of the Long Walk on Snow Hill stands the Copper Horse, a bronze statue surmounted by the figure of George 111. Apparently the maker of the statue forgot to include one of the stirrups and, in disgrace, killed himself. However, if one visits the statue today, neither stirrup is seen and there is no record of a ghost at the statue itself.

Which brings us to Herne's sightings. Although Herne has been used by parents as a bogeyman to scare their children, the number of authenticated cases of encounters with him are few and far between. The earliest date we have is, of course, the 14c. when tradition has it that the Herne episode took place. Although other monarchs are mentioned, it is Richard II who is most popularly associated with Herne. He was born in 1367, ascended the throne in 1377 and was murdered by Henry IV in 1400. The son of the Black Prince, he reigned at a period of great social unrest which included the Peasants' Revolt of 1381 against the poll tax, led by Wat Tyler and put down by Richard with a firm hand. He made no bones about the fact that he wished to abolish government by Parliament and he turned out to be an unjust king who was given to extravagance. It is perhaps fit that such a monarch should have been plagued by the ghost of Herne. According to the story Herne was seen again after Richard's death, but there are no records of these sightings, unless we include Ainsworth's story of his appearance to Henry VIII and of course Shakespeare's reference in the late 16c.

A Fiendish Phantom

From here there is a long gap until we hear from the author Hector Bolitho in his book "The Romance of Windsor Castle", published in 1946. One passage tells of a man whom he met once walking through the Great Park who told him that when he was a schoolboy at Eton he heard the sound of Herne's horn and hounds. It is difficult to pinpoint the date here, but perhaps we could guess a date in the first decade of this present century. Shortly after, around 1910, the Hon. Evan Baillie is reputed to have had a "close encounter" of a kind when he too heard Herne's horn and hounds. Unfortunately, these are the only details we have and his son, Lord Burton, was unable to provide any further information. Nikolai Tolstoy, in his book "The Quest for Merlin", tells of a friend of his, the poet Charles Richard Cammell, who informed him that when he was a schoolboy at Eton before the First World War, he often talked with an old keeper who had himself seen Herne on his wild chase. Before we continue, however, we must mention a royal connection. Joan Forman, in her "Haunted Royal Houses", confides that a member of the present Royal Family confirmed to her that Herne has been seen this century. Thus, insubstantial though some reports may be, here we have a royal assent as to at least one sighting, wherever and whenever it occurred.

Herne's hounds have been heard over a wide area from Winkfield through Windsor to Old Windsor and it is at the latter place that our next story takes place. In 1926 Mrs Walter Legge, apparently a level headed person who was also a J.P., was living at Farm House at which place she records two encounters with Herne. On the first occasion she had just gone to bed when she heard the baying of hounds which appeared to come from the direction of Smith's Lawn, the sound getting louder until it died away in the direction of the Castle. Almost two weeks later she heard them again, this time at precisely midnight, and on this occasion she was not alone, for her daughter too, heard what she described as "strange sounds, almost like Herne the Hunter's hounds". The two women had just returned from London and were standing outside the house briefly before retiring. It appears that they heard the hounds travel towards the Copper Horse from the direction of Bears' Rails. What is convincing about these two reports is the time, for who would be hunting so late at night but Herne? Mrs. Legge and her

A Fiendish Phantom

The next case brings us to 1962 and involves a group of youths. One version records that whilst in the Great Park one night, they found a hunting horn and, at the edge of a clearing, one of them blew it. To their surprise there was an answer from another distant horn and then they heard the sound of the hounds coming towards them. Shortly after Herne himself appeared mounted on a black horse, at which the terrified youths dropped the horn and ran.

However, there is another version which ends in tragedy and involves two youths from Windsor and a teddy boy. On this particular day they went out into the Great Park obviously up to no good and began to break down young trees. The teddy boy, however, suddenly stopped and picked up what looked like a hunting horn and showed it to the other two, who looked at him a bit oddly. One of the Windsor youths then told him to drop it and to run for it, whereupon the teddy boy began to feel a bit uneasy. Nevertheless bravado overcame him and he blew it and in reply there came a terrifying yell from the trees and they all heard the baying of hounds. All three immediately ran for their lives, but the teddy boy couldn't keep up with the other two and he stumbled as he heard feet chasing after him. The Windsor youths finally arrived at a church and ran in where they stopped and saw their friend struggling on. He arrived just in front of the church door when they heard the sound of an arrow flying though the air and the teddy boy screamed and then fell dead in the church porch. But the two youths saw no sign of the hunter, his hounds nor an arrow. This account has parallels with other similar tales and, as such, continues the tradition of a very old theme.

The following encounters with Herne both involve soldiers. It appears that sentries at the Castle have been haunted by Herne for hundreds of years. When sighted, it was said that the soldiers would quickly tell the locals, for his appearance brought death to cattle and blight to crops and trees. The first is a short account concerning a young recruit of the Grenadier Guards whose ghost haunts the Long Walk. According to the tradition he is said to have shot himself because he saw Herne, but presumably he had had time to tell someone about the sighting! A few weeks later, his ghost was seen by a guardsman on duty, who saw the daughter lived here for many years afterwards, but never again heard the ghostly hounds.

The next encounter, again from the 1920's, provides us with the only detailed sighting of what can only be Herne the Hunter, although it took place at Cookham Dean which used to be at the edge of Windsor Forest in times gone by. It was a summer's evening when another(!) level headed woman was crossing the common on her way back from posting a letter. Part way across the common she became aware that her two dogs appeared to be frightened and instead of running on ahead they cowered behind her. It was then that she saw a man emerge from the undergrowth, but it was no ordinary man for upon his head he wore a set of antlers. She was not afraid, however, and instead of continuing on her way decided to follow the figure which crossed the common and she saw it walk into one of three oak trees which grew at the edge of the common, whereupon it disappeared. This story is significant in two respects, the first being its importance as an authentic Herne sighting. The second reason is the site where he disappeared, i.e. at an oak tree which, as we have already seen in Chapter 2, is highly relevant when discussing Herne. All in all a fascinating account.

It is also a noteworthy fact that if one stands at Stirlings Barn at Cookham Dean, the midwinter sun is seen to rise over Windsor Castle's Round Tower and that if this line is extended it runs through the site of Herne's Oak. Similarly, the midsummer sunset can be seen over Cookham Dean from the Round Tower. If not a ley line, then this appears to be an alignment of some significance.

Moving on to the 1930's, there were apparently a number of sightings made during this decade including one made by some workmen who were engaged upon renovations at the Castle. Another incident involved a woman who lived in Windsor and who said that she both heard and saw Herne's hounds run across an open space in the Park one bright moonlit night. On another occasion, in 1936, the hounds were not seen but were heard by two Eton schoolboys who heard an invisible hunt in full cry gallop towards them. Although they saw nothing, they reported feeling an icy blow as the unseen figures rushed past them.

A Fiendish Phantom

figure of his dead colleague in the bright moonlight. When he returned to quarters, he discovered that the sentry he had previously relieved had also had a similar experience.

The second story involves another young Coldstream guardsman who was on duty at the East Terrace of the Castle in September of 1976. It appears that he was found unconscious by his relief who could not bring him round. After being taken to the garrison's medical centre, he eventually regained consciousness when he told of a strange apparition he had witnessed. He informed his adjutant that he had been performing his guard duty as normal when his eyes fell upon one of the statues in the Italian Garden. He said that as he looked at it the statue began to grow horns and suddenly came to life ! (Whether the horns were antlers is not stated.) It was at this point that he fainted.

The adjutant blamed the guardsman's experience on stories he had heard from older soldiers. He was of the opinion that, based in such a lonely spot in the middle of the night with nothing else to do, it was not surprising if the imagination played funny tricks. He added that "Whether he saw something or whether it was all in the mind is anyone's guess".

A Windsor woman who contacted the local newspaper about the incident was convinced that it was Herne who had materialised : "This guardsman, poor devil, might have seen something....He might be in trouble". She added that her grandmother told her 60 years ago of sightings of Herne. Buckingham Palace dismissed the idea altogether stating that they had never heard of a ghost at Windsor Castle, which is strange considering that a number of ghosts are said to haunt the Castle. Henry V111 haunts the Deanery, Elizabeth I the Royal Library, Charles 1 the Canon's House and George 111 has been seen in the room where he spent his last years, suufering from madness.

A Castle historian pointed out, however, that Herne has never been seen at the Castle itself, but only in the Forest. He also recalled a not unrelated tale. One cold winter's night many years ago, a young soldier was standing guard at the Castle. It seems that the Dean of Windsor

A Fiendish Phantom

took pity on him and brought him a bowl of hot gruel to warm him up. Unfortunately, when the guardsman saw a cloaked figure approaching him, he panicked and fired, just missing the poor clergyman! His punishment was 20 lashes.

However, returning to 1976, a spokesman at the Victoria Barracks said that there would be no charge in the case of this latest incident on the East Terrace. Nevertheless, it appears that the sentry never recovered from his terrifying experience and it is said that he is now a gibbering wreck, unable to come to terms with what he saw. The East Terrace is especially prone to hauntings and an incident from the last century involved another guardsman. On duty one night he saw a strange creature resembling an elephant and, being very frightened, he shot at it. The bullet went straight through the apparition, which suddenly vanished.

Another strange manifestation was observed from the East Terrace in 1783, the year that Herne's Oak produced its last acorns. Three eminent men, amongst others, reported in the northeastern sky the sighting of what we should now call a U.F.O. At about 9.45 p.m. a brilliant spherical object was observed moving along eastwards. It subsequently grew more oblong and split up into a trail of smaller bodies each with a tail, before vanishing towards the south-east. An explosion was heard shortly after. It seems that the East Terrace is not a place to be at night if you are of a nervous disposition. However, it is not open to the public and so the only persons likely to see these phantoms are the Royal Family or those unfortunate young guardsmen.

There is a further tale not unconnected with the Herne's Oak ley line which is worth repeating here. This concerns Henry James (Senior) who, in May 1884, was staying at Frogmore Cottage situated in what is now the Home Park. After a satisfying family dinner one day, he was sitting alone in front of the fire, in a good state of mind and free from worries. All of a sudden he was overcome with fear and he trembled all over. He felt that the cause of his terror was a shape of some sort which was emanating evil and sitting invisibly in the room. Within about ten seconds he had been reduced from a sane, contented human being to a nervous wreck. Although diagnosed by doctors as being under stress due to overwork, he was insistent that he was in perfect health physically and mentally. Colin Wilson, who recounts the event in his "Mysteries", suggests that James may have come into contact with an elemental and that this was connected in some way with the ley which passed close to the cottage. If this was the case, perhaps Herne is only one of many otherworldly spirits which manifest themselves in the near proximity of leys. It seems clear that certain locations do attract either benign or evil vibrations. And so this sighting brings us up to date with encounters with Herne, tantalizing as some of them are.

This is not the end of the Herne story, however, since there is a strange tale yet to relate, much of which I am thankful to Michael Bayley for the details. It concerns a stone head discovered in the garden of the old vicarage opposite the parish church in Windsor High Street. The original building was given to the parish by William Evingdon in 1487 "for the good of his soul". This Evingdon was the last Keeper of the Great Park and was therefore a kind of successor to Herne himself. It

The Mask of Herne
(Courtesy of Michael Bayley)

was during the moving of the vicarage to Park Street in the early 1930's that workmen dug up what came to be known as the "Mask of Herne the Hunter".

The head depicts the face of a man sporting a fine moustache, with deepset eyes set beneath a fierce looking brow and bearing ears which can only be described as those of an animal, not unlike a deer's. But what is interesting to us is the antlers which are growing out of the top of his head. The overall effect is that of a mixture of the green man faces which adorn many of our churches and the grotesque figures which are found on the outside of cathedrals put there to ward off evil spirits. It therefore looks as though it may well have adorned some religious or other building in the past, although Mr. Bayley has his own theory as to its origin. He believes that, as it was made in such a way as to allow it to be hung up, it was an emblem of some kind. His conclusion is that it stood for the job of Keeper of the Great Park, which allowed him to be the only person other than the king to hunt deer in the Park and which explains why it was found where it was.

Mr. Bayley's father acquired the head not long after it was found, but the vicar claimed it back in the late 1930's and it did not come back into public notice until it was rediscovered after the Second World War in the garden at Park Street. When this property was due to be sold, the head found its way into the church museum where it remained until 1963. It was at this time that Mr. Bayley's views on Herne and his Mask appeared in the local press and a week after publication the church was broken into and the Mask stolen, never to be seen again. It seems likely that it was taken by a cult group who believed that they had got hold of an ancient likeness of the horned god Cernunnos. They could not have been more wrong for as we have seen, it is probably of 15c. date or it may even have been Victorian. One expert decreed that it was made of loadstone, a hard type of artificial stone used during Victorian times, but Mr. Bayley, a qualified architect, does not accept this interpretation and places it firmly in the 15c.

This would have been the end of the story except for the fact that it has a kind of sequel, in the form of a very unusual tale which will not seem relevant until we reach the end. One morning in September 1856 two little boys, William Fenwick and William Butterworth, were standing on a street corner in Windsor when they were offered a lift by a man driving a light horse and carriage. They accepted and were driven to Albany Road, not far from Park Street, where they became drowsy and woke up at about 5.30 p.m. remembering nothing at all. However, they were no longer in Albany Road but at Victoria Bridge in the Home Park.

Upon contacting the police they gave detailed descriptions of the driver, his horse and his carriage, but no trace could be found of them. Initially the police thought that the boys may have been drugged by some unbalanced person, but later they wondered whether the boys had imagined the whole episode. However, many years later when he was living in London, an acquaintance showed William Fenwick a photograph of the Mask of Herne after it had been dug up. Bearing in mind that he was now over eighty and the kidnapping incident had taken place when he was about eleven, he had no doubt that the face he now saw was that of the driver who drove him and his friend off to Albany Street all those years ago. So have we here an appearance of Herne the Hunter in another guise? Who can tell?

Stone heads have long been used either to ward off evil powers or to act as guardians over a sacred spot. Their importance dates back to Celtic times, when the iron age peoples revered the head and believed that severed heads had magical properties. The heads of their enemies were thrown down wells, buried beneath temples or hung outside the gates of their hillforts. The Celtic scholar Dr. Anne Ross tells of a strange experience involving two Celtic stone heads from Hadrian's Wall which she had been asked to examine. She took an instinctive dislike of them, but placed them in her study. A couple of nights later she woke up in the middle of the night feeling afraid and to her horror caught a glimpse of a tall figure leaving her room. She felt somehow that it was part animal, part man but felt she had to follow it. But even though she saw it in a downstairs corridor, it vanished.

A few days later she returned home with her husband at about 4.00 p.m.

A Fiendish Phantom

only to find her teenage daughter in a state of shock. Having arrived home from school, she had seen something "huge, dark and inhuman" on the stairs which had jumped down over the banisters and landed in the corridor. She also felt she had to follow it, but when she looked for it, it had again vanished. After similar experiences, Dr. Ross finally connected the occurrences with the heads and gave them back to the museum (see footnote). Perhaps this is the reason why the Mask of Herne had been buried since it, too, attracted unknown forces, but such happenings also tend to occur with those who are sensitive to such powers and we can only wonder what happened after the Mask's theft.

We have seen Herne and his ghostly hunt appearing in various places with varying kinds of apparitions and noises. He is said to have been seen as far away as Twyford in Berkshire, where a ghostly rider has been recognised by some as Herne. This is quite feasible since Windsor Forest did once extend out that far. But perhaps the most well known cases of local sightings in the Windsor area have been at times of national crisis. This type of appearance, where a ghost heralds some form of disaster, is quite common and the scenario of the castle being haunted by a ghost who appears just before the death of the lord is a common theme of ghost stories. A good example of a legend of this type concerns Charlborough Park, six miles north of Wareham in Dorset, and the ancestral home of the Drax family. It is said that, whenever a white stag appears in the deerpark, this means that the birth of an heir to Charlborough is due in the near future.

A real life example is recalled by the incident described by Lord Lindsay who recounted what happened to his friend William Wardlaw Ramsay. Whilst crossing the valley of the Wady Arabia the latter saw a band of horses and riders amongst the sandhills and it was apparent that there could have been no horsemen in the area. In the Middle East such apparitions are regarded as portents foretelling the death of whoever saw them, which proved to be the case with Ramsay since he died a few

---

Footnote: It has been claimed that these heads were made in the 1950's, but it does not detract from the very real experiences which occurred.

weeks later.

Nearer home and nearer Herne, the shouts of the Wild Huntsman were heard as he rode across the sky on the eve of Henry IV's murder in 1413. Whether it was Herne himself it is not possible to say, but Henry IV was the man who ordered the killing of Richard II, to whom the Herne story happened. Perhaps it was the first sighting of Herne the Hunter after the demise of Richard II, for it was not to be until he died that Herne would resume his hauntings. Apparently the Wild Hunt was also seen in France on the eve of the French Revolution in 1789, and we have already encountered Wild Edric warning England of an imminent war.

In recent years, there have been a number of sightings which occurred just before a crisis in Britain. Herne was said to have appeared just before the Depression in 1931 (when he appeared along with a white stag and the ghostly form of the oak), before the abdication of Edward VIII in 1936, before the outbreak of the Second World War in 1939 and before the death of George VI in 1952. In the latter instance an observer records walking down Windsor High Street on 6th February of that year and hearing the Sevastopol Bell in the Round Tower ringing, which only occurs when there is a royal death. The news of the King's decease had just been received and the remarks of a passing woman are here worth reporting. She was heard to say, "I knew some dreadful tragedy had happened, for Herne the Hunter was seen again in Windsor Great Park last night". There does not appear to have been an appearance before the disastrous fire in 1992, however.

Thus we come to the end of Herne's hauntings or do we? There is no reason to think that he should not appear again, for he seems to make not infrequent appearances, either by himself or with his Wild Hunt. Although there is no doubt that he exhibits features of the racial memory type of ghost, in his case that of the horned leader of the Wild Hunt, he does also appear to incorporate other facets. His appearances before national disasters are a relatively recent manifestation, but perhaps this represents a modern rationalisation of a phenomenon, i.e. the Wild Hunt, which had lost its relevance to a 20th. century

A Fiendish Phantom

population. So, although to some extent he can be categorized, he refuses to be completely pinned down and I am sure that there is really no other ghost like Herne the Hunter.

The Web of Herne

The search draws to a close and it is time to try to unravel the threads which make up the legend of Herne the Hunter. As we have seen in the foregoing chapters, there are several distinct elements contained within the legend and perhaps it will clarify the situation if the key elements are listed.

1. Antlers - Cernunnos.
2. The Wild Hunt - Ghostly Appearances.
3. Woden - Self-sacrifice.
4. The Oak - World Tree.

First it can safely be said that if it were not for the phenomenon of the deer's yearly growth of a new set of antlers, then the legend of Herne would not have taken its present shape. Symbolising as they do regeneration and fertility, they impressed ancient man at an early stage of development so much so that they came to mean something very special. As we have seen, men were donning antler headdresses as long ago as, perhaps, 25,000 years and the Sorceror cave painting comes down to us as a strange beast-man perhaps imbued with renewed energy and power from the antlers he wears. He is Lord of the Animals, presiding over the other creatures upon which early man depended. As Nikolai Tolstoy puts it, such a figure was "the guardian of the hunting culture, a being who looked after the welfare of animals and apportioned game among hunters worthy of his beneficence". And surely it is this idea which lies at the ultimate root of the legend, Herne in many ways resembling this primitive individual, skilled as he was in the matters of woodcraft and the hunt. Prehistoric man had a natural affinity with the rest of creation and lived his life, including the hunting of game, within the context of a kind of ecological spirituality, which industrialised man has lost.

For the immediate precursor of Herne, however, which in itself owes much to the palaeolithic hunters, we must look to the Celtic god Cernunnos. As described earlier, antlered gods were not uncommon in

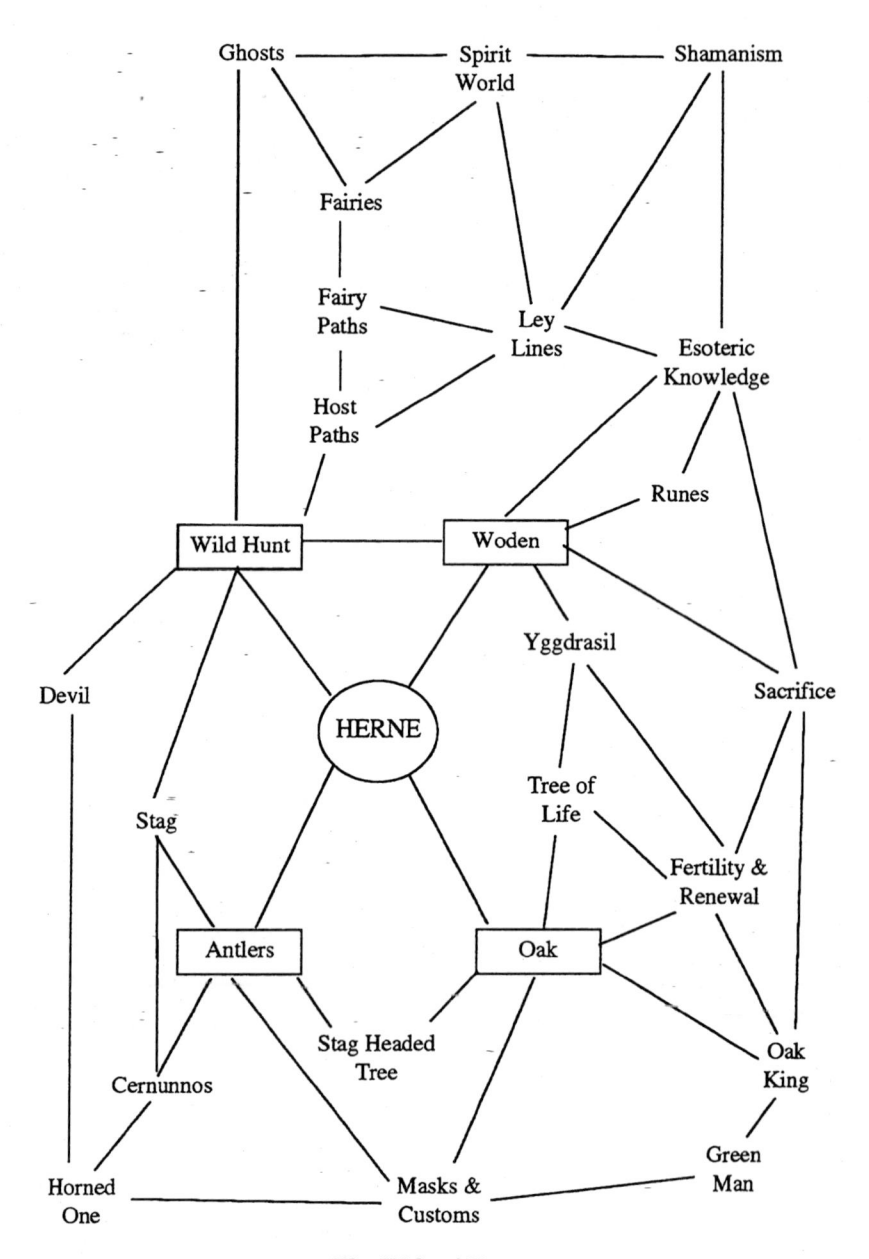

The Web of Herne

The Web of Herne

the ancient world, but owing to his popularity on the Continent and in Britain, Cernunnos holds a special place in the formation of Herne as a figure. That the horned god was a cult in Britain, its worship continuing through the Roman period, is significant and it is not impossible that devotion to such a god may well have survived the coming of Christianity. It is entirely likely that, even if worship had ceased, then the horned one would have stayed alive in folk memory and folk tales. The arrival of the pagan Saxons may well have prompted a revival of such cults, which had not been in the open since the Christianisation of the Roman Empire, and the horned god could have merged with beliefs and mythological characters from the Saxon pantheon. In fact it has been pointed out that there was a marked degree of similarity between the Celtic and Germanic peoples, especially with regard to religious practices. For example Germanic tribes would often sacrifice spoils of war and deposit valuable articles as offerings in pools or streams, a practice well known in the Celtic world. Classical authors describe the two peoples in much the same vein and both lived adjacent to each other in the heavily forested areas of northern Europe. It is not insignificant that tree worship was important to both cultures. Perhaps we see a local cultural fusion at Windsor, with its sacred mount and oak groves, which kept alive the idea of the horned one and giving rise ultimately to the legend of Herne.

The Saxons, of course, bring us to that strange personnage Woden, the one-eyed, the hooded, the wise, the self-sacrificer and leader of the Wild Hunt. As we have discovered, gods and goddesses, especially in the Romano-Celtic worlds, were equated with each other, the Romans often calling native deities by Latin names, having linked them because of similar attributes. Thus it is possible that this also happened when the Saxons intermingled with the Romano-Britons. Woden we have described as hanging on the World Tree and the sacrifices made in his honour have their counterparts in Celtic customs. As Wild Huntsman he is at one with Gwynn ap Nudd from Welsh tradition, which is a remnant of the Celtic culture which covered the whole of Britain before the arrival of the Romans and Saxons. Herne is without a doubt a leader of the Wild Hunt and his antecedants are to be found in both the Celtic and Germanic traditions. Woden was also a fertility god and the continental versions of the Wild Hunt sometimes depict him pursuing females. Petry suggests that Herne may have had a reputation as a lover amongst the Windsor locals, which would not be surprising since two versions of his legend contain sexual elements. Fertility again brings us back to the ancient symbolism of antlers and to the power of nature, the abundance of game to hunt, the Lord of the Animals and so to Cernunnos. We can therefore see the web of connectedness between all these disparate ideas which all lead to the figure of Herne.

The idea of sacrifice and renewal were concepts ingrained into the minds of pre-Christian pagans and indeed they were incorporated into the belief system of the new religion. Thus Herne's death and rebirth as a reinvigorated spirit is a theme which would have taken hold of the imaginations of succeeding waves of peoples who have inhabited our land. He is connected with the tradition of the everlasting battle between the oak-king and holly-king, that eternal round of death and rebirth as winter follows summer. This is the stuff of folk tradition and legend, many of whose tales can be traced back to age-old themes.

That there are many customs and traditions carried on into modern times for which the original purpose has been long forgotten is beyond doubt. So such customs as mummers' plays, maypole dancing and dressing as hobbyhorses can be seen as deriving from pagan rites which aimed at propitiating the ancient gods and spirits. Even walking under a ladder can be traced back to the idea that ladders were made from wood and therefore contained a tree-spirit which must not be upset. The magic of numbers is especially potent still, the number seven being of considerable importance. Odd numbers particularly were thought to have occult significance and the number three ranked almost as highly as seven. Three was considered lucky in both pagan and Christian societies, in the latter case probably because it denoted the Trinity. Accidents and deaths were expected to occur in threes, which shows that it was ill luck as well as good luck that was signified. In Celtic times everything was done in threes, as it featured as their sacred number. Many of their deities had three aspects and the number linked these gods and goddesses to legends and tales in which Celtic poets enjoyed making use of ingenious play with numbers and letters. That

Lindow Man died a triple death tells us that this was no mere accident.

The number three turns up twice in the Herne legend. Firstly, there are the three presents given to Herne by the King the hunting horn, the silver chain and the purse of money. Secondly, there are three main characters Herne, the King and Urswick. It can surely be no coincidence that this theme of the number three occurs in a legend which we have already found has close links with Celtic beliefs. The veneration of the number three is not unknown in Germanic culture also, for instance Woden was one of three brothers and the Northern goddesses of fate, the Norns, were three in number. They were three sisters who went under the names of Urd, Verdandi and Skuld, being personifications of past, present and future. Apart from weaving the web of fate, their task was to sprinkle daily the tree Yggdrasil with water and to place fresh clay around its roots. Yggdrasil possessed three main roots, one in Asgard, home of the gods, one in Midgard, the world of men, and one in Niflheim, the underworld. And thus we arrive back at the World Tree and another link with Germanic mythology. The similarities between the two cultures, Celtic and Germanic, are again emphasised and providing us with further evidence for the foundation of the origins of the Herne legend.

As to the incorporation of more far-flung influences such as the Balkan figure of Heron, not much can be said with certainty. The fact that he was associated with hunting, death and snakes does sound convincing up to a point. It may well be that the Romans' interest in him may have added to the melting pot of mythology and folklore which has resulted in the composite individual we now know as Herne the Hunter, as does the possible connection with the heron, the bird. However, I feel that Cernunnos is the origin of Herne's name, despite the fact that he is only one, although a very important one, of several elements which make up the nature of Herne.

I have already suggested the possibility of there having once been a custom in Windsor involving a stag's mask, although this is obviously mere speculation. But it may help explain the persistence of the legend and perhaps an antlered figure played a part in a kind of mummers' play many centuries ago. A king, wizard, doctor and other strange characters are not unusual figures to find in folk plays and the theme of the Herne legend is so universal that it is not at all impossible that this may have once been the case.

What is certain, however, is the folklore which surrounds the oak tree, and its importance in ancient times has been commented on. Also material is the connection with royalty, such as Charles II, and therefore we should not be surprised to find the two concepts together in one story. The oak has a long history of being specially important to Berkshire and we have seen how in fact this significance may have emanated from the Windsor area. What is not in doubt is the fact that a tree was long known as Herne's Oak and had a considerable tradition attached to it, just as did so many others throughout Britain. What makes Herne's Oak so special, however, is the age of the legend which Shakespeare confirms dates back to at least the 16c. and, which I think I have shown in this book, probably dates back much further. As to the connections of the oak with stags and antlers which appears in such stories as those of Herne, William Rufus and the Hartshorn Tree, perhaps the origin lies in the annual cycle of regeneration. Red deer antlers begin to grow anew in May at precisely the time the oak is in flower and, given the similarity of antlers to the branches of a tree, it is likely that the two were considered together as representing the sun's peak of power and intensity.

This association dates back far into prehistory, the depiction of antlers in conjunction with sun symbols being found at various sites in Europe. At Tajo de las Figuras in Spain is a rock shelter which contains a neolithic carving portraying a circular sun image with rays in the form of antlers. A later carving, this time from the bronze age, occurs at Val Camonica in Italy and depicts stags whose antlers meet in a solar symbol. And from Petersfield in Hampshire we come across a Celtic coin showing the head of Cernunnos with a sunwheel set between his antlers. The circle and cross are examples of the various ways in which the sun has been represented for many thousands of years. Most other types are variants of these, such as flowers and the swastika, the latter being common in ancient Europe. A Romano-Celtic altar discovered in the Pyrenees exhibits a swastika in association with a tree. Thus it is apparent that the sun's waxing and waning was linked in the prehistoric mind with trees losing and growing their leaves and stags shedding and regrowing their antlers. Herne's Oak, the midsummer tree, is therefore one aspect of a mythical conception which cannot be separated from the antlers and the dying midwinter sun which form the basis of the seasonal theme of Herne's story.

The idea of tree spirits may well be the origin of ghostly appearances in and around forested areas and some would say that these are associated also with energies from ley lines. Ghosts, of course, have featured in history since the beginning of time and Herne is only one of many strange apparitions which have been encountered and reported over the centuries. What we have with Herne, however, is something different. It is not just a matter of classing him as a mere ghost, as I hope the contents of this book have shown. Herne, I feel, could only have occurred in Britain, where the specific mix of ancient cultures have provided a background for the appearance of a figure of this type. We have seen that his appearances are traditionally during the winter, but that in this century he is associated with times of national crisis. This change is in itself very unusual in ghosts who normally haunt to a fixed, unchanging timetable. But, as our search reveals, Herne is no ordinary ghost.

Ghosts, wild hunts and folktales are all examples of humankind's contact with, and an unconscious need of, an otherworldly realm. They put us in touch with another order of reality which all peoples of the world have experienced, some more than others and which, despite our materialist world, refuses to go away. Tales of old often strike a chord in our psyche and recurrent themes occur in many different tales around the globe.

An unexpected rendering of the Herne legend surfaced in the 1970's with a series of Western novels by John J. McLaglen. Entitled Herne the Hunter, they tell of the exploits of a gunslinger named Jed Herne, described as a violent man in a violent land whose story takes place in a succession of books (over a dozen) advertised as a savage western series. "Jed Herne was a shootist: a man who lived by the gun: he was Herne the Hunter". He gained his nickname due to a trail of vengeance which he embarked upon in the early stories, in which he hunted the murderers of his wife and killed them one by one, no matter how long it took nor what obstacles crossed his path. Titles of the novels emphasise their violent nature and include White Death, River of Blood, Death in Gold, Death Rites and Massacre. Other than the ideas of hunting and dying, however, the similarity between Jed Herne and the Windsor Herne ends, but it is of note to see his name used in such a way and, who knows, perhaps it has brought some new adherents to the legend and other folklore from the islands of Britain.

British folklore is especially rich, inheriting elements from as far back, perhaps, as the neolithic age, but certainly incorporating aspects from the various "invaders" of these isles the Celts, Romans, Saxons, Vikings and Normans. All have added a particular slant to the melting-pot of ideas, beliefs and superstitions which make up the British outlook, be it in the sphere of politics, religion or folklore. The legend of Herne the Hunter is a prime example of the fusion of traditions from many centuries, some specific and some recurring.

Mythical tales have enjoyed a revival in recent years, as a perusal of the science fantasy shelves in any bookshop will reveal. The book which, perhaps, began this revival was Tolkien's "Lord of the Rings" an epic which drew heavily from Germanic and Celtic mythology. Since then such sagas have proliferated and fantasy is becoming more popular than science fiction. This represents, I feel, a reaction to the type of society we now find ourselves in, with the collapse of traditional religion. The predictions of science fiction once held out hope or provided warnings for the world to come, but since science has now been found to be unable to bring us Utopia, then people are turning inwards to such disciplines as the New Age movement and the quests, magic and mysticism to be found in fantasy novels. However, the ideas behind these stories are not new and the interested seeker will find much to capture his imagination in investigating ancient myths like the Greek, Celtic and Germanic, and delving into mysteries such as the Grail quest in the Arthurian legends.

The Web of Herne

And now we must bring this search to a close, and I think that we have been able to disentangle a number of threads which go to make up what I feel is the composite figure of Herne. We have weaved our way in and out of a number of ideas and have visited many sideroads on route and I hope that a better understanding of Herne has been achieved, one that has incorporated all the multifarious facets of his nature. Perhaps Ainsworth did embellish his story somewhat and invented certain elements, but the themes that he used were certainly relevant, and I am sure that he would not have been unaware of them. As to Herne's future, I shall be very surprised if he does not manifest himself again, but whether it will be to those unfortunate guardsmen or only to psychics, who can tell? The durability of his legend is assured, however, and I am sure that tales of Herne the Hunter will be told for some time yet.

APPENDIX A

As mentioned in chapter 2, Herne's Oak was inadvertently felled during the reign of King George 111. An ode to the demise of the tree was published in the Whitehall Evening Post:

Upon Herne's Oak Being Cut Down in the Spring of 1796

   Within this dell, for many an age,
     Herne's Oak uprear'd its antique head -
   Oh! most unhallow'd was the rage
     Which tore it from its native bed!

   The storm that stript the forest bare
     Would yet refrain this tree to wrong,
   And Time himself appear'd to spare
     A fragment he had known so long.

   'Twas marked with popular regard,
     When fam'd Elizabeth was queen;
   And Shakespeare, England's matchless bard,
     Made it the subject of a scene.

   So honour'd when in verdure drest,
     To me the wither'd trunk was dear;
   As, when the warrior is at rest,
     His trophied armour men revere.

   That nightly Herne walk'd round this oak,
     'The superstitious eld receiv'd';
   And what they of his outrage spoke,
     The rising age in fear believ'd.

Appendix A

The hunter in his morning range,
  Would not the tree with lightness view;
To him, Herne's legend, passing strange,
  In spite of scoffers, still seem'd true.

Oh, where were all the fairy crew
  Who revels kept in days remote,
That round the oak no spell they drew,
  Before the axe its fibres smote?

Could wishes but ensure the power,
  The tree again its head should rear
Shrubs fence it with a fadeless bower,
  And these inscriptive lines appear; -

'Here, as wild Avon's poet stray'd' -
  Hold! let me check this feeble strain -
The spot by Shakespeare sacred made,
  A verse like mine would not profane.'

Local historian Michael Bayley has in his possession a piece of wood from this original Herne's Oak, given to him by the great, great, great granddaughter of one of the foresters who chopped it down, each man being allowed to keep a chip for himself (see photo).

Herne's Oak has subsequently been replaced twice, the first time in the incorrect place by Queen Victoria and later by her son Edward V11, which stands to this day. The commemorative plaque which is placed nearby reads as follows :

> THIS TREE WAS PLANTED 29TH. JANUARY 1906 BY COMMAND
> OF HIS MAJESTY THE KING EDWARD V11 TO MARK THE ORIGINAL
> POSITION OF "HERNES OAK".
>
> IN 1796 THIS OAK, BEING DEAD, WAS CUT DOWN WITH OTHER
> DEAD TREES IN THE PARK AND ITS NAME WAS TRANSFERRED
> TO ANOTHER OLD OAK STANDING A FEW PACES TO THE SOUTH.

Appendix A

> THE SECOND "HERNE'S OAK" WAS BLOWN DOWN 31ST. AUGUST 1863 AND IN ITS PLACE A NEW TREE WAS PLANTED BY HER MAJESTY QUEEN VICTORIA 12TH. SEPTEMBER 1863.
>
> IN REPLANTING THE AVENUE IN 1906 THE NEW TREE HAD TO BE REMOVED.
>
> ITS COMMEMORATIVE INSCRIPTION HAS BEEN RESET ON THE BACK OF THIS STONE.

The earlier inscription contained the information in paragraph three of the above, together with the first four lines from Mistress Page's account of Herne in "The Merry Wives of Windsor", quoted at the beginning of chapter 1.

The second Herne's Oak blew down as described and the news was sent to Queen Victoria, who was in Germany at the time. She immediately commanded that nothing was to be done with the trunk, and until she returned a watch was kept on it night and day. When she arrived back in Windsor, she visited the spot along with other members of the royal family. She apparently stuck to the theory that this was indeed Herne's Oak and had the Royal Upholsterer, a certain Mr. Goetz, make mementos such as chairs, cabinets and worktables from the tree. There is still in existence a three volume set of the complete works of Shakespeare bound in wood from this tree. A receipt for this reads "binding wood from Herne's Oak £3 3s.", and the cover is engraved with "Herne's Oak blown down in the Home Park, August 31, 1863".

It is not possible for the public to visit Edward V11's Herne's Oak as it is in the private section of the Home Park just north of Frogmore. The house and gardens of Frogmore are open at selected times each year, where Queen Victoria's mausoleum and the graves of other royal personnages, including Edward V111, can be visited. For liquid refreshment, however, the Herne's Oak public house at the little village of Winkfield, 5 miles south west of Windsor town centre can be recommended (leave Windsor via the A332 or B3022).

APPENDIX B

We have seen how Herne has been depicted in literature via Shakespeare and Ainsworth and now it is the turn of poetry in the form of a poem by Eric Mottram, which is a graphic evocation of the Herne Legend.

Windsor Forest   *Bill Butler in Memoriam*

1.

holly thickness projected impervious
a yard before him pleasurable difficulties
a blue stream from bushes footed twisted snakes between
roots leapt a wild spectral humanity

    deer skins around tawny gaunt limbs
    he his a skull helmet antlered

    phosphoric fire cut in links
    rusted from his left arm chain

    on his right wrist a horned owl
    dilated taloned erect

    red balled   feathers angered
    in full cauldrons the moons
laughed pooled below his oak
        glades vistas beyond lightening the scathed branches
crime called heinous lay unknown inside a tale
        his haunt created by his body self-hung
        vengeance a night-rider interventions
a wood demon controls forest traces between night growth
        a hunt ghost in green spirit
his branches the oak's demon tines
        a free owl flies before his two black dogs
        moonlit skin at a water edge
        his glare   their fang-tuned heads
        above dead ripples
from a calix horn smoke poured into his lips to vanish him
        he left deer imprints and beyond
long glades vistas a moon glitter the eyes' lake in slow banks trees assemble

Appendix B

    Amergin sings questions after claims
                I am a stag of seven tines
                who set out letters in ogham
                twice seven high royal top
                the chalk mask in honour
                Beth's birth turns the year
                    his own oak openings: I am god who sets the head
                    afire in Duir
he begins each year and turns each year at seven
              searches Sun control
              strides into flame on John's Day
              leg by leg into the year door
              he has guarded
              Llyar sea guard for seafaring

the oracular oak a beech they found   phegos   the oak king   fagus
spotted stag of the wood
                Actaeon
                    as a cloud occludes a beech opens
                    under three strikes

            'changed and renewed
            from their withered state'
            entangled oak tops
                  the beech book by an oak seer
the goodluck bat drifts above such moonlight snakes
                  can glide from the trunk rift
                  he starts from the brake
                  the spectre rides hart royal
his skin gypsy swarthy peers through the network of the haye
            where a trapped buck he lay panted regal
            tines gored their flesh nets and he's out
            twenty flash horsemen behind his flint-locked hoof
            the dripping trees   chain flies out from his neck
            blue flame from horn
                  light unearth settled on rigid trees
Snow Hill sleeps under the owl wheel
                  a gull against the smacking tide
                  no live sound
                  as his crevice opens
                  snake laughs and the crested green hero calls
an errand in wilderness   his hand a vice his gaze a long black veil
                  his mouth opens to a cave home
his conditions out of green sod tempt the Christian earls
unproof to demonic grasp extinguishing light

Appendix B

Sir Thomas Wyatt came to   unbandaged in a hewn sandstone hill
tree pillared   torchlight water
an altar thrown hewn boulder his antler candled head
      'some tyme I fled the fyre that me brent
      by see, by land, by water and by wynd'
now he follows druid fire   'mashed in the breers that erst was to torne'
closes hands with Herne's chase his hounds Saturn and Dragon
vaulted up on neither saddled nor bridled horse sable
      uttered a wild cry
      plunged into the surface
      rose gleaming streams and the moonlight owl
      at the entrance
a gourd flask for pledges he imposes spirits for the chase
Sir Thomas drinks to see beast trees excited by the hart and hunts with Herne
                                      on Hawk's Hill

            the hart's head dismembered
            he places his skull inside the hart's
            his blood in deer spirits gone again
            the king's man in shaken impotence
            hunts his part
to where the hollow roars flame at the oak base
            slow earth falls in
            electric fluids drench the castle
'the very hounds with which thou hunted me shall lick thy blood!'

                          2.

Expert beyond us in woodcraft
                  he could rear a wild boar
                  dig a badger unkennel a fox
                  bay a marten vent an otter
                  fly a falcon
antler gored he entered his vista
                  'a hurt from hart's horn bringeth to the bier'
to cure a bleeding skull is bound to his head by leather
            the king hung gold links around his neck
            his lost craft and gained thunder laughter
            took to roots and compelled homage
            in the scathed oak kingdom

Appendix B

   debts scattered seed in men collected at their prime
        dread-master cased in green steel
       love knifed to conquest
         you shall accompany me on my midnight rides
         the unutterable excitement of the chase
         threaded moonlight on tangled grove
         swim in pleasure
         absolute queen feared
his offer for committed crimes   a liberation into power
       I have known no human passion except hatred and revenge
       alone at the head   a numerous band
      since love shrank to oaths upon an altar throne
      I may be in league with darkness
      but I have no wish to aid him
      Take care of your soul your own way
      or my obedience binds skull to nerve
      tined antennae to the moon
on occasion he appeared as a monk in dark second skin
     it suits a figure of dark corners
     hims in arch Windsor
     changes in tree light
the hood helms his leather cure
from castle chamber to chamber
stone walls to thickets
deeds to move through

          records in beech books where you may read
          oak energies   a plunge into transforming distances
          hunt horns
          calls
          the allegiances

                                                 1977

APPENDIX C

It is little known that Herne the Hunter has been the subject of an opera. "Herne. A Legend of Royal Windsor" in three acts comprised a libretto by Edward Oxenford, music composed by John Old and was first performed at Reading Town Hall on 14th. December, 1887. The version of the tale adopted in the work involved Herne's love for a nun, whom he killed in a fit of jealousy.

Apparently the work was a great success, as a long review in the Berkshire Chronicle confirmed. The account included a lengthy description of the action, which can be summarised : Herne appeared in the ballroom of Windsor Castle and carried off Lady Constance, the bride of Lord L'Estrange, in defiance of King Henry V111 and his guards. He took Constance to a ruined chapel, in which hung the portrait of a nun and, being struck by the resemblance to his victim, after an exultant "Mine!", he left her imprisoned. The Lady, however, is eventually rescued from the clutches of the demon hunter and married to her lover, the celebration of the marriage concluding the work.

The legend of Herne the Hunter was sung during the opera by Mr. Henry Guy, who played L'Estrange :

L'Estrange :   'Tis nigh two hundred years ago,
        That Herne the Hunter to the Crown,
And none so deft with spear and bow,
        As he who still enjoys renown.

He'd bring to earth the fleetest hind,
        Defy the fiercest boar at bay,
Train up the hawk, the bugle sound,
        Unearth the fox, the badger slay.

But soon a gentler task arose
        He sought to win a maiden's heart;

Appendix C

                Of love he felt the keenest throes,
                    And bared his breast to Cupid's dart.

                The maid he loved was vowed to God,
                    A nun within a convent nigh;
                Yet from the holy paths she trod,
                    He wean'd her feet, alas! to die!

                For soon, in a fit of jealous rage,
                    He slew the maid he loved so well;
                And in remorse, the sinner's wage,
                    A self-made gift to death he fell.

Chorus :   Yes, on that withered oak he died,
                A murderer and a suicide.

L'Estrange : And since the day he joined the dead,
                He roams at night the forest land,
                With antlers on his ghostly head,
                Surrounded by a phantom band....

Chorus :   O! monstrous fiend, from depths infernal,
                May thy tortures be eternal.

The reviewer was obviously much taken with the performance, which featured a first class band and a well drilled chorus. It apparently abounded with dramatic situations, of which the music was admirably descriptive, but the reviewer considered that although Mr. Otto Fischer, who played Herne, sang "The Lord of the Forest am I" with spirit and power, he was a little out of tune at times!

I am sure that it must have been a very enjoyable evening and there was loud applause after the opera's finale. There would have been many encores, but it seems that as well as the heavy scoring of the work, the music was too exacting on a first night's performance. Whether it has been heard since I have not been able to ascertain. Perhaps now is the time for a revival.

APPENDIX D

Herne's importance assumes cosmic proportions when the following tale, which seems to be current belief in certain esoteric circles, is told. (Reference Prediction magazine March 1990).

It commences with the star Sirius B, a white dwarf which is the smaller member of the double star system which includes the brightest star in the sky Sirius itself, better known as the Dog Star in the constellation of Canis Major. Apparently advanced beings known as the Cosmic White Brethren are said to have their origins on Sirius B, or more precisely on a planet orbiting the star. It was from here that they journeyed to Earth and it was from amongst their company that Herne the Hunter himself is said to originate.

Herne the Hunter, evoked second son of the Lord Herne, or Cernunnos, was incarnated from Sirius B to Brittany, together with his hunting band, the White Stags or Hounds of Herne. Their purpose was to track down a renegade White Brother who had rebelled with other so-called Black Brethren in a heavenly war. This search took them to Britain and then to Ireland, thus giving us the legend of the Wild Hunt and its leaders such as Herne at Windsor. There is a mythological connection here with the myth of Actaeon, who was hunted down and killed by his fifty hounds. As we have seen, Robert Graves tells us that Actaeon was a sacred king of a stag cult who was killed at the end of his fifty month reign, which is interesting because Sirius B orbits the larger Sirius A every fifty years. So here we have yet another thread in Herne's web and perhaps some of us are attached to it as well, for it is

----

Footnote: The theme of this appendix is enlarged, along with much more, in Robert K.G. Temple's fascinating book "The Sirius Mystery", which suggests answers to the question of how an African tribe knew that Sirius was in fact a double star. His theory implies that perhaps the tribe preserved knowledge acquired from beings who travelled to Earth from the Dog Star.

Appendix D

suggested that mankind was seeded over from Sirius millennia ago. Therefore it is possible, it is said, that any one of us, in another life, may have been a member of Herne the Hunter's band.

Make of this what you will, it will no doubt appear very strange to many readers. What this story tells us, however, is the continuing fascination that Herne and his legend have for people of varying backgrounds and beliefs.

APPENDIX E

Herne, Cernunnos or the Horned One is a figure which has been subject to a revival in recent years amongst neo-pagan and occult groups. Nicholas Mann tells us that as Green Man, Lord of the Animals, Wild Man or Horned God he is the Hunter God who becomes the prey he hunts. As he dies annually he willingly enters the Underworld and becomes God of Earth before rising again, and this yearly cycle reveals him as the Star Son and Serpent Son in turn. The passing of his spirit into the soul of other beings, like the stag, enables him to acquire the secrets of life and death. As Serpent Son he is embraced by the Goddess and rules over the dead half of the year but is given birth to by the Goddess come Spring as the Star Son. Together the God and Goddess represent the cycle of the seasons and the sharing of life itself with the rest of creation, an idea which is echoed in the philosophy of the green movement. The God and Goddess complement each other and symbolise the partnership that is required for a balanced and harmonious existence on this planet.

In magical working it is apparently useful to know that Herne's sign is Taurus, his colour is green and his emblems a bow, a white stag and the moon. Herne the Hunter is not easily invoked and, during meditation, a hunter figure only normally appears when one is spiritually troubled or was a hunter in a previous incarnation.

Herne is popular amongst modern day witches who practise the ancient craft of Wicca. Being a religion based on Nature and the seasonal rhythms, it is not difficult to understand why Wicca has adopted Herne as its tutelary male deity. He epitomises the life-force and rules over the cycles of life, death and rebirth, and covens' ceremonies often reflect these attributes. Indeed, the preferred ritual headgear of the High Priest is often the horned crown. Janet and Stewart Farrar describe in "The Witches' God" a Herne/Cernunnos ritual as an initiation for a male witch as well as giving details on how to make Herne incense using deer's tongue leaves amongst other ingredients.

Appendix E

And finally Herne is invoked. Rhiannon Ryall, in her book entitled "West Country Wicca : A Journal of the Old Religion" (1989) describes a chant used at the festival of Samhain. Moving clockwise round the ritual circle, the men chant the following rhyme, a fitting end to our search for Herne the Hunter.

Iron clad the meadows,
Hoar frost covers all.
Weasel slithers whitely,
Black rooks give call for call,
Fox shadows on the hillside,
Hunters Moon it swings on high,
The Wild Hunt is out now,
Winds through the chimney's sigh.
Herne comes awalking
While the Lady takes her rest.
Loving, warm and gentle,
White dove within her nest.
Herne comes astriding,
On Dolmen, Tor and hill,
Sees the hunter and the hunted,
In sky and field and rill.
Herne he comes aleaping,
His Kingdom hard and cold,
But all are his own ones,
The frightened, shy or bold.
Herne he does his making,
His minding and his sending,
He cares for all in this Realm,
And in the next one tending.
Death is but a doorway,
Herne is on both sides,
Here or there don't matter,
Old Herne with us abides.

LIST OF DATES

B.C.

c150000 - c30000	Neanderthal man (see Chapter 4)
c100000	Burial of boy with antlers in Jebel Qafzeh cave, Israel
c20000	Palaeolithic cave paintings (The Sorceror)
c8500	Mesolithic age commences (Star Carr antler headdresses)
c4500	Neolithic age commences (ritual antler deposits)
c2000	Bronze age commences (reverence of the oak first recognised)
c700	Iron age (Celtic) commences (worship of Cernunnos, the horned god)

A.D.

43	Roman invasion of Britain (worship of Heron, the Thracian rider)
c450	First Saxons in Britain (worship of Woden)
c530	Caesarius of Arles deplores those who wear animal skins and the heads of horned beasts
c700	Theodore, Archbishop of Canterbury, condemns those who dress in animal skins
793	First Vikings in Britain (worship of Odin/Woden)
915	Regino of Prun's proclamation against the wearing of animal masks
1023	Burchard of Worm's proclamation against the wearing of animal masks
1091	Sighting of the Wild Hunt by a priest in France
1100	William Rufus killed (Herne parallel)
1127	Sighting of the Wild Hunt at Peterborough
1154	Sighting of King Herla and his Wild Hunt
1283	Sighting of the Wild Huntsman near York

List of Dates

1377	Richard II ascended the throne (and later encountered Herne)
1400	Death of Richard II (and recommencement of Herne's hauntings)
1413	The shouts of the Wild Huntsmen heard on the eve of Henry IV's murder
c1450	The Mask of Herne created
c1525	Rycharde Horne's illicit hunting in Windsor Forest
1597	Shakespeare's "Merry Wives of Windsor" first performed
1783	Herne's Oak bears acorns for the last time
1789	Herne's Oak bears leaves for the last time
1789	Sighting of the Wild Hunt in France on the eve of the Revolution
1796	Herne's Oak felled (Herne's hauntings cease)
1843	W. Harrison Ainsworth's novel "Windsor Castle" published
1854	Sighting of Wild Edric prior to the Crimean War
1863	Erroneous Herne's Oak blown down and replaced by Queen Victoria
1887	First performance of the opera "Herne. A legend of Royal Windsor" in Reading
1906	Herne's Oak II planted (Herne's hauntings recommence)
c1907	Eton schoolboy hears Herne's horn and hounds
c1910	Hon. Evan Baillie hears Herne's horn and hounds
1926	Mrs. Walter Legge twice hears Herne's hounds
c1927	Herne seen by a woman at Cookham Dean
1931	Appearance of Herne before the Depression
c1933	Discovery of the Mask of Herne
c1935	Herne seen by workmen renovating Windsor Castle
1936	Herne's hounds heard by two Eton schoolboys
1936	Appearance of Herne before the abdication of Edward VIII
1939	Appearance of Herne before World War II
1952	Appearance of Herne before the death of George VI

List of Dates

1962	Herne appears to youths in the Great Park
1963	Disappearance of the Mask of Herne$
1972	Publication of first book on Herne the Hunter (Herne the Hunter: A Berkshire Legend by Michael John Petry)
1976	Last publicised sighting of Herne to a Castle guardsman (see Chapter 8)
1981	Publication of a book of poems on the subject of Herne (A Book of Herne by Eric Mottram)
1994	Publication of this volume

BIBLIOGRAPHY

Alexander, Marc — Haunted Castles (1974)
Alford, Violet — The Hobby Horse and Other Animal Masks (1978)
Ashe, Geoffrey — Mythology of the British Isles (1990)
Barham, Tony — Witchcraft in the Thames Valley (1973)
Baring-Gould, S. — A Book of Folklore
Bernheimer, Richard — Wild Men in the Middle Ages (1952)
Bolitho, Hector — The Romance of Windsor Castle (1946)
Bord, Janet & Colin — Earth Rites (1982)
Branston, Brian — Gods of the North (1955)
Branston, Brian — The Lost Gods of England (1957)
Brown, Raymond Lamont — A Book of Superstitions (1970)
Brown, Raymond Lamont — A Casebook of Military History (1974)
Burl, Aubrey — Rites of the Gods (1981)
Burl, Aubrey — The Stonehenge People (1987)
Campbell, Joseph — Primitive Mythology (1968)
Cavendish, Richard — The Black Arts (1967)
Cawte, E.C. — Ritual Animal Disguise (1978)
Clark, J.G.D. — Excavations at Star Carr (1954)
Cleaver, Alan (Ed.) — Strange Berkshire (1986)
Collins, Andrew — London Walkabout (1984)
Collins, Andrew — Would the real Herne the Hunter please stand up (Albion's Sacred Heritage no. 9, 1991)
Dames, Michael — The Avebury Cycle (1977)
Dames, Michael — The Silbury Treasure (1976)
Dash, Mike — Accidental Death of an Anti-Christ (Fortean Times No. 48, 1987)
Davidson, H.R. Ellis — Gods and Myths of Northern Europe (1964)

Bibliography

Devereux, Paul	Earth Lights Revelation (1989)
Dixon, William Hepworth	Royal Windsor, Vols. 1-4 (1879/80)
Ekwall, Eibert	The Concise Oxford Dictionary of English Place Names (1960)
Farrar, Henry	Windsor: Town & Castle (1990)
Farrar, Janet & Stewart	The Witches' God (1989)
Forman, Joan	Haunted Royal Houses (1987)
Forman, Joan	The Haunted South (1978)
Foss, Michael (Ed.)	Folk Tales of the British Isles (1977)
Frazer, J.G.	The Golden Bough (1922)
Gimbutas, M.	The Goddesses and Gods of Old Europe (1982)
Gooch, Stan	Guardians of the Ancient Wisdom (1979)
Graves, Robert	Greek Myths (1960)
Graves, Robert	The White Goddess (1952)
Green, Miranda	The Sun-Gods of Ancient Europe (1991)
Hadingham, Evan	Secrets of the Ice Age (1979)
Hamel, Frank	Human Animals (1915)
Harrison, Michael	The Roots of Witchcraft (1973)
Hedges, J.W.	Tomb of the Eagles (1984)
Hedley, Oliver	Windsor Castle (1967)
Hill, B.J.W.	Windsor and Eton (1957)
Howey, M.D.	The Horse in Magic and Myth (1923)
Hughes, Pennethorne	Witchraft (1965)
Hutton, Ronald	The Pagan Religions of the Ancient British Isles (1991)
James, E. O.	Sacrifice and Sacrament (1962)
Jung, C.G.	Memories, Dreams, Reflections (1963)
Lofthouse, Jessica	North-Country Folklore (1976)
MacCann, P.	Celtic Mythology (1983)
MacNaghten, Angus	Haunted Berkshire (1986)
Mann, Nicholas R.	The Keltic Power Symbols (1987)
Maringer, J.	The Gods of Prehistoric Man (1956)
Merrifield, Ralph	The Archaeology of Ritual and Magic (1987)
Mitchell, Anne	Ghosts along the Thames (1972)

Bibliography

Mosley, Charles	The Oak: Its Natural History, Antiquity and Folklore
Mottram, Eric	A Book of Herne (1981)
Murray, Margaret	The Witch Cult in Western Europe (1923)
De Nablick, A.J.	Wild Deer (1959)
Newman, Paul	Gods and Graven Images: The Chalk Hill Figures of Britain (1987)
Oesterley, W.O.E. & Robinson, T.H.	Hebrew Religion (1937)
Oliver, Sue	Sirius B - Cradle of the Gods? (Prediction, March 1990)
Petry, Michael John	Herne the Hunter: A Berkshire Legend (1972)
Phillips, Guy Ragland	Brigantia (1976)
Radford, E. & M.A.	Encyclopedia of Superstitions (1961 revised Christina Hole)
Readers Digest	Folklore, Myths and Legends of Britain (1973)
Rice, M.A.	Abbots Bromley (1939)
Ripley, Robert L.	The Omnibus Believe it or Not!
Ross, Anne and Robins, Don	The Life and Death of a Druid Prince (1989)
Rowan, John	The Horned God (1987)
Rowling, M.	The Folklore of the Lake District (1976)
Ryall, Rhiannon	West Country Wicca (1989 and 1993)
Shackley, Myra	Neanderthal Man (1980)
Shackley, Myra	Wildmen (1983)
Squire, Charles	The Mythology of the British Isles (1905)
Stewart, R.J.	The Underworld Initiation (1985)
Stewart, R.J.	The Waters of the Gap (1981)
Taylor, Ian	The Giant of Penhill (1987)
Taylor, Rogan	Who is Santa Claus? (Sunday Times feature, 21/12/1980)
Tighe, R. & Davis J.	Annals of Windsor, Vols 1 & 2 (1858)
Tolstoy, Nikolai	The Quest for Merlin (1985),
Tongue, Ruth L.	Forgotten FolkTales of the English Counties (1970)

Bibliography

Watson, Lyall	Heaven's Breath (1984)
Whitlock, Ralph	The Oak (1985)
Wilson, Colin	Mysteries (1978)
Wilson, Colin	The Windsor Horror (The Ley Hunter no. 118, 1993)
Berkshire Mercury	12/8/1971
The Ley Hunter	Nos. 116 -119 (1992/93)
Windsor Express	25/1/1963
Windsor Express	1/2/1963
Windsor Express	23/7/1971
Windsor Express	1/10/1976

A selection of other titles from Capall Bann:
Available through your local bookshop, or direct from Capall Bann at: Freshfields, Chieveley, Berks, RG16 8TF.

West Country Wicca - A Journal of the Old Religion By Rhiannon Ryall

This book is a valuable and enjoyable contribution to contemporary Wicca. It is a simple account of the Old Religion. The portrayal of Wicca in the olden days is at once charming and deeply religious, combining joy, simplicity and reverence. The wisdom emanating from country folk who live close to Nature shines forth from every page - a wisdom which can add depth and colour to our present day understanding of the Craft. Without placing more value on her way than ours, Rhiannon provides us with a direct path back to the Old Religion in the British Isles. *This is how it was*, she tells us. *This is the way I remember it.* Both the content of what she remembers and the form in which she tells us, are straightforward, homespun and thoroughly unaffected.

"West Country Wicca is a real gem - it is the best book on witchcraft I have ever seen! Thank you Rhiannon Ryall for sharing your path with us." - Marion Weinstein

ISBN Number   1 89830 702 4   Price £7.95

The Call of the Horned Piper by Nigel Aldcroft Jackson

This book originated as a series of articles, later much expanded, covering the symbolism, archetypes and myths of the Traditional Craft (or Old Religion) in the British Isles and Europe. The first section of the book explores the inner symbology and mythopoetics of the old Witchcraft religion, whilst the second part gives a practical treatment of the sacred sabbatic cycle, the working tools, incantations, spells and pathworking. There are also sections on spirit lines, knots and thread lore and ancestral faery teachings. Extensively illustrated with the author's original artwork. This is a radical and fresh reappraisal of authentic witch-lore which may provide a working alternative to current mainstream trends in Wicca.

ISBN Number   1-898307-09-1   Price £8.95

The Sacred Grove - The Mysteries of the Tree By Yvonne Aburrow

The veneration of trees was a predominant theme in the paganism of the Romans, Greeks, Celtic & Germanic peoples. Many of their rites took place in sacred groves & much of their symbolism involved the cosmic tree; its branches supported the heavens, its trunk was the centre of the earth & its roots penetrated the underworld. This book explains the various mysteries of the tree & explains how these can be incorporated into modern paganism. This gives a new perspective on the cycle of seasonal festivals & the book includes a series of rituals incorporating tree symbolism. "The Sacred Grove" is the companion volume to "The Enchanted Forest - The Magical Lore of Trees, but can be read in its own right as an exploration of the mysteries of the tree.

ISBN Number 1 898307 12 1   Price £10.95

Angels & Goddesses - Celtic Paganism & Christianity
by Michael Howard

This book traces the history and development of Celtic Paganism and Celtic Christianity specifically in Wales, but also in relation to the rest of the British Isles including Ireland, during the period from the Iron Age, through to the present day. It also studies the transition between the old pagan religions & Christianity & how the early Church, especially in the Celtic counmtries, both struggled with & later absorbed the earlier forms of spirituality it encountered. The book also deals with the way in which the Roman Catholic version of Christianity arrived in south-east England & the end of the 6th century, when the Pope sent St. Augustine on his famous mission to convert the pagan Saxons, & how this affected the Celtic Church.. It discusses how the Roman Church suppressed Celtic Christianity & the effect this was to have on the history & theology of the Church during the later Middle Ages. The influence of Celtic Chhristianity on the Arthurian legends & the Grail romances is explored as well as surviving traditions of Celtic bardism in the medieval period. The conclusion on the book covers the interest in Celtic Christianity today & how, despite attempts to eradicate it from the pages of clerical history, its ideas & ideals have managed to survive & are now influencing New Age concepts & are relevent to the critical debate about the future of the modern chrurch.

ISBN 1-898307-03-2   Price £9.95

Auguries and Omens - The Magical Lore of Birds   By Yvonne Aburrow

The folklore & mythology of birds is central to an understanding of the ancient world, yet it is a neglected topic. This book sets out to remedy this situation, examining in detail the interpretation of birds as auguries & omens, the mythology of birds (Roman, Greek, Celtic & Teutonic), the folklore & weather lore associated with them, their use in heraldry & falconry & their appearances in folk songs & poetry. The book examines these areas in a general way, then goes into specific details of individual birds from the albatross to the yellowhammer, including many indigenous British species, as well as more exotic & even mythical birds.

ISBN Number 1 898307 11 3   Price £10.95

The Pickingill Papers - The Origin of the Gardnerian Craft by W. E. Liddell
Compiled & Edited by Michael Howard

George Pickingill (1816 - 1909) was said to be the leader of the witches in Canewdon, Essex. In detailed correspondence with 'The Wiccan' & 'The Cauldron' magazines from 1974 - 1994, E. W. Liddell, claimed to be a member of the 'true persuasion', i.e. the Hereditary Craft. He further claimed that he had relatives in various parts of southern England who were coven leaders & that his own parent coven (in Essex) had been founded by George Pickingill's grandfather in the 18th century. There is considerable interest in the material in the so-called 'Pickingill Papers' & the controversy still rages about their content & significance with regard to the origins of Gardnerian Wicca. This book provides, for the first time, a chance for the complete Pickingill material to be read & examined in toto together with background references & extensive explanatory notes. Topics included in this book include the origin of the Gardnerian Book of Shadows and Aleister Crowley's involvement, the relationship between the Hereditary Craft, Gardnerian Wicca & Pickingill's Nine Covens, the influence of Freemasonry on the medieval witch cult, sex magic, ley lines & earth energy, prehistoric shamanism, the East Anglian lodges of cunning men, the difference between Celtic wise women & the Anglo Saxon cunning men. It also includes new material on the Craft Laws, the New Forest coven, Pickingill's influence on the Revived Craft & a refutation of the material on Lugh & his basic thesis in Aidan Kelly's recent book 'Crafting the Art of Magic'.

ISBN Number 1 898307 10 5   Price £9.95

The Inner Space Work Book By Cat Summers & Julian Vayne

A detailed, practical book on psychic and personal development using the Tarot, pathworkings and meditations. The Inner Space Work Book provides a framework for developing your psychic and magickal abilities; exploring techniques as varied as shamanism, bodymind skills and ritual, through the medium of the tarot. There are two interwoven pathways through the text. One concentrates on the development of psychic sensitivity, divination and counselling, as well as discussing their ethics and practical application. The second pathway leads the student deeper into the realm of Inner Space, exploring the Self through meditation, pathworking, physical exercises and ritual. Both paths weave together to provide the student with a firm grounding in many aspects of the esoteric. Together, the pathways in The Inner Space Work Book, form a 'user friendly' system for unlocking all your latent magickal talents.

ISBN 1 898307 13 X   Price £9.95

Pathworking 2nd Ed. By Pete Jennings & Pete Sawyer

A pathworking is, very simply, a guided meditational exercise, it is sometimes referred to as 'channelling' or 'questing'. It is used for many different aims, from raising consciousness to healing rituals You don't have to possess particular beliefs or large sums of money to benefit from it & it can be conducted within a group or solo at time intervals to suit you. This book teaches you how to alter your conscious state, deal with stress, search for esoteric knowledge or simply have fun & relax. It starts with a clear explanation of the theory of pathworking and shows in simple & concise terms what it is about and how to achieve results, then goes on to more advanced paths & how to develop your own, it also contains over 30 detailed and explained pathworkings. Highly practical advice & information is given on how to establish and manage your own group. No previous experience is assumed.

ISBN Number   1 898307 00 8   Price £7.95

Celtic Lore & Druidic Ritual By Rhiannon Ryall

Rhiannon Ryall is well known for her book 'West Country Wicca'. This new book brings some of the inner mysteries to those interested in the Pagan Path or Tradition. Inevitably the Druidic Path crosses that of any genuine Gaelic Tradition of Wicca, so this book contains much druidic lore.. Background material pertaining to the Druids is also included as this explains much of their way of viewing the world and it enables the reader to understand more fully their attributions in general and their rituals in particular. The book is divided into five parts:

1: Casting circles, seasonal sigils, wands, woods for times of the year, Celtic runes, the Great Tides, making cones and vortices, polarities and how to change them, the seasonal Ogham keys and some Ogham correspondences. 2: Old calendar festivals and associated evocations, the "Call of Nine", two versions of the 'Six pointed Star Dance', Mistletoe Lore, New Moon working,the Fivefold Calendar. 3: Underlying fundamentals of magical work, magical squares and their applications, more use of Oghams, the Diamond Working area. 4: Five initiations, including a shamanic one, some minor 'calls', some 'little magics'. 5: Background information on the Celtic path, the Arthurian myth and its underlying meaning and significance, the Three Worlds of the Celts, thoughts regarding the Hidden Path, some thoughts and final advice. A veritable treasure trove for anyone interested in the Celtic path.

ISBN 1 898307 225   Price £9.95

Other titles from Capall Bann

A detailed illustrated catalogue is available on request, SAE or International Postal Coupon appreciated. Titles are available direct from Capall Bann, post free in the UK (cheque or PO with order) or from good bookshops and specialist outlets.

Animals, Mind Body Spirit & Folklore

Angels and Goddesses - Celtic Christianity & Paganism by Michael Howard
Arthur - The Legend Unveiled by C Johnson & E Lung
Auguries and Omens - The Magical Lore of Birds by Yvonne Aburrow
Book of the Veil The by Peter Paddon
Call of the Horned Piper by Nigel Jackson
Cats' Company by Ann Walker
Celtic Lore & Druidic Ritual by Rhiannon Ryall
Compleat Vampyre - The Vampyre Shaman: Werewolves & Witchery by Nigel Jackson
Crystal Clear - A Guide to Quartz Crystal by Jennifer Dent
Earth Dance - A Year of Pagan Rituals by Jan Brodie

Earth Magic by Margaret McArthur
Enchanted Forest - The Magical Lore of Trees by Yvonne Aburrow
Healing Homes by Jennifer Dent
Herbcraft - Shamanic & Ritual Use of Herbs by Susan Lavender & Anna Franklin
In Search of Herne the Hunter by Eric Fitch
Inner Space Workbook - Developing Counselling & Magical Skills Through the Tarot
Kecks, Keddles & Kesh by Michael Bayley
Living Tarot by Ann Walker
Magical Incenses and Perfumes by Jan Brodie
Magical Lore of Animals by Yvonne Aburrow
Magical Lore of Cats by Marion Davies

Magical Lore of Herbs by Marion Davies
Masks of Misrule - The Horned God & His Cult in Europe by Nigel Jackson
Mysteries of the Runes by Michael Howard
Oracle of Geomancy by Nigel Pennick
Patchwork of Magic by Julia Day
Pathworking - A Practical Book of Guided Meditations by Pete Jennings
Pickingill Papers - The Origins of Gardnerian Wicca by Michael Howard
Psychic Animals by Dennis Bardens
Psychic Self Defence - Real Solutions by Jan Brodie
Runic Astrology by Nigel Pennick
Sacred Animals by Gordon 'The Toad' Maclellan
Sacred Grove - The Mysteries of the Forest by Yvonne Aburrow
Sacred Geometry by Nigel Pennick
Sacred Lore of Horses The by Marion Davies
Sacred Ring - Pagan Origins British Folk Festivals & Customs by Michael Howard
Secret Places of the Goddess by Philip Heselton
Talking to the Earth by Gordon Maclellan
Taming the Wolf - Full Moon Meditations by Steve Hounsome
The Goddess Year by Nigel Pennick & Helen Field
West Country Wicca by Rhiannon Ryall
Wildwood King by Philip Kane
Witches of Oz The by Matthew & Julia Phillips

Capall Bann is owned and run by people actively involved in many of the areas in which we publish. Our list is expanding rapidly so do contact us for details on the latest releases. We guarantee our mailing list will never be released to other companies or organisations.

Capall Bann Publishing, Freshfields, Chieveley, Berks, RG20 8TF.